Praise for **SAFELIGHT**

"Shannon Burke's accomplished and haunting debut is a minimalist tour de force. . . . *Safelight* tells a surprisingly potent story."
—*The New York Times Book Review*

"A powerfully visual, oddly intimate experience . . . with cinematic, unflinching clarity . . . [Burke] has made brilliant metaphoric use of the photographic medium . . . to reveal the strange, healing beauty that can be found at the heart of ugliness and despair."
—*San Francisco Chronicle*

"Pitch-perfect dialogue and [a] feel for male camaraderie give [*Safelight*] an electric charge. . . . Burke's evocation of a murky world, where savior and sinner come in one macho package . . . makes this an exhilarating standout."
—*Kirkus Reviews* (Best Books of 2004)

"Edgy and hip . . . fast-paced."
—*The Orlando Sentinel*

"Burke is a deft writer. . . . Vivid dialogue and sharply rendered street scenes keep the pages turning."
—*Time Out New York*

"Burke's remarkable debut, which will arrest readers from the first paragraph, is direct, crisp, and cinematic, its prose matching the unadorned and chilled landscape in which the story takes place. Even with its minimalist quality, the novel manages t̶ ̶ ̶ ̶ ̶e reader with unexpected swells of f̶ ̶l̶

"[A] dark, tender debut . . . Burke's spare prose and sharp eye for the beauty in urban misery make this a moving tale of lost souls searching for permanence in a chaotic world."

—*Publishers Weekly*

"*Safelight,* Shannon Burke's novel of paramedics and violent death in New York's tougher quarters, is provoking and disturbing. How could it be otherwise? What is startling and unexpected, however, is that despite the unblinking, bloodstained photorealism of its reportage, *Safelight* is above all a work of nerveless intelligence, disarming tenderness, and hard-won optimism."

—JIM CRACE

"A powerful, hypnotic, and strangely beautiful vision of hell on earth. Burke's voice floats out over our hemisphere amid the distinctive strains of Denis Johnson, Raymond Carver, and Frederick Exley. But in the end, his frequency is all his own. A fearless debut."

—GARY SHTEYNGART

"There is a dark side in all of us and Shannon Burke is not afraid of it. In *Safelight,* he explores our all-too-human instincts without pity, condescension, or romance. He creates characters who are real, who feel, and who make us feel—and he does so with formidable grace. This book will make you cry. But it will be worth it."

—ALLISON GLOCK

"Burke immerses the reader in the urgent world of emergency medicine. Using photography sometimes as his weapon, sometimes as his moral eye, paramedic Frank Verbeckas explores the blurred lines between victim and victimizer, the criminal and the cop, as well as his own difficult past. *Safelight* is a stunning debut novel about what it is to be human, to feel."

—A. M. HOMES

SAFELIGHT

SAFELIGHT

A Novel

Shannon Burke

Random House Trade Paperbacks New York

2005 Random House Trade Paperback Edition

Copyright © 2004 by Shannon Burke
Reading group guide copyright © 2005
by Random House, Inc.

Published in the United States by Random House Trade Paperbacks,
an imprint of The Random House Publishing Group,
a division of Random House, Inc., New York.

RANDOM HOUSE TRADE PAPERBACKS and colophon
are trademarks of Random House, Inc.

Originally published in hardcover in the United States
by Random House, an imprint of
The Random House Publishing Group,
a division of Random House, Inc., in 2004.

LIBRARY OF CONGRESS CATALOGING-IN-PUBLICATION DATA
Burke, Shannon.
    Safelight : a novel / Shannon Burke.
        p.   cm.
    ISBN 0-8129-7174-4
        1. Young men—Fiction.   2. Terminally ill—Fiction.
3. Fathers—Death—Fiction.   4. Harlem (New York, N.Y.)—
Fiction.   5. Emergency medical technicians—Fiction.   I. Title.
    PS3602.U7555S34 2004
    813'.6—dc22   2003069549

Printed in the United States of America

www.atrandom.com

9 8 7 6 5 4 3 2

Book design by Casey Hampton

SAFELIGHT

Ugliness was the one reality. The coarse brawl, the loathsome den, the crude violence of disordered life, the very vileness of thief and outcast, were more vivid, in their intense actuality of impression, than all the gracious shapes of Art, the dreamy shadows of Song.

OSCAR WILDE

Compassion is perhaps the chief and only law of human existence.

FYODOR DOSTOYEVSKY

"I don't know."

1

She came into view at the top of the stairway and motioned to hurry us. Burnett, who wasn't going to hurry for anyone, kept climbing at the same indolent pace. We found her on the third floor in an open doorway. Beyond her, an empty room—white walls, folded canvas tarps, a dried roller, stacked cans. I smelled paint.

"We here for you?" Burnett asked.

"No. Him," she said.

She shifted her eyes toward a shut door at the end of the newly painted white room. Burnett walked past her.

"Locked," she said. "It's locked."

Burnett tried the knob, put his shoulder into it, then stepped back.

"What caliber?"

"I don't know. Like this . . ."

She showed the length of the gun with two hands.

"Whatta you think?" he asked. "He ever tried before?"

"I don't know."

"You see him load it?"

She shook her head.

"Well, this is stupid. Don't go near the door."

That was it for Burnett. He walked to the end of the hall-way, jerked the window open, and felt for cigarettes. She leaned against the doorframe and watched him sullenly. I thought I ought to say something.

"It's not our job," I said. "Some barricaded patient. What're we gonna do?" Then, "You're his girlfriend?"

"I hardly know him. I'm part of his group."

"Group?"

"I'm positive," she said.

I didn't understand what she meant. Then I did.

She looked as if she was just out of college. Brown hair partway down her back, olive skin, a navy pullover sweat-shirt with dangling white cords coming out of brass sealed eyelets. With her shy demeanor, thin, nervous mouth, big eyes, and scrawny body, she wasn't particularly attractive. The dispatched report said her name was Emily Pascal.

"What's his count?"

"Ten. So he's got nothing to lose," she said.

We could hear sirens, far away at first, then closer. Down the hallway, Burnett stood with two hands on the window-sill. Emily Pascal leaned off the doorframe.

"Don't go in there," I said.

"I just want to check," she said. "Before the cops. Maybe he'll go willingly."

She started into the apartment, into the newly painted

room. I reached out as if to restrain her but she gave me a sharp look.

"Don't touch me."

I pulled my hands away. Burnett glanced over, bored.

"Don't let her in, Frank."

But she'd already gone in. Then two things happened, one right after the other. The sirens outside the window wound down and stopped and in the sudden, unexpected silence afterward there was a loud pop from the inner room. I heard something fall.

"I don't fucking believe it," Burnett said.

He tossed his cigarette out the window and started back, not hurrying at all. He joined me in the doorway. The girl, Emily Pascal, now lay on her side, making little moaning noises. Her right leg was out straight, but her left leg was bent, and around the left knee I saw a hole in her jeans about the size of a pea. Around that hole there was a growing purplish stain.

2

Burnett stepped directly over the girl and walked to the door. Ran his finger around a little hole. Put his eye to it.

"This's just too perfect," he said. "This's six months of day care. This's French class for toddlers." He knocked on the shut door of the second room. "You got'm?"

I said I did.

I tried the knob and was surprised when it turned. The

guy must have unlocked it just before he shot himself. A surprisingly considerate last gesture. The door opened inward, then came up against something solid—his head. I peered around to see his body at an angle and his arm to the side. The kid had fired with his left hand into the left side of his forehead. The entrance, which was only a small hole, was almost hidden in his hairline. The exit wound, at the back of his head, was about the size of a child's fist. On the inner surface of the door there was a splash of blood mixed with bone. I knew I only had a minute, so I couldn't waste any time. I locked the door, took a camera from my breast pocket, and began taking pictures. Of his slumped body. Of his head. Of his face. Of his blank eyes. Of the entrance wound. The exit. The left hand that still gripped the .38 loosely. The brilliant splash on the newly painted white door. I heard the cops in the front room. I took a close-up of the gun as one of the cops tried the knob. I unlocked the door, put the camera away, and was feeling for a pulse when one cop stuck his head in. Then they all came in, three of them—officious, gruff. One, two, three, they stepped over the oblong puddle. One murmured something, a joke I didn't hear. Another had a notepad and was writing with particular intentness. I gave the time of pronouncement and stepped into that front room where the girl lay on her back, keeping herself very still, hissing when Burnett got close to her leg. The bullet had entered just below the kneecap and deflected downward, never going more than a quarter-inch beneath the surface of the skin. As I entered, Burnett said, "Where'd he take it?"

"Left temporal."

"DOA?"

I said it was. Burnett had cut the girl's pants to the thigh. He looked down at the wound, which he had not bandaged.

"I left this."

"Now?" I asked.

I could hear the cops talking on the other side of the door.

"Aw, they don't give a fuck," he said.

I took eight or nine photographs of the girl: a close-up of the entrance wound just below the kneecap, a closer shot of the bullet visible as a lump beneath the skin, a bullet hole in the door, a long shot with Burnett kneeling next to her and some paint cans stacked in the corner. In all of these photographs Emily Pascal looked bewildered. You couldn't really blame her for that. Five minutes before we'd been talking idly, waiting for the police to arrive. Now her friend was dead, she was shot in the shin, and a paramedic was hovering over her eagerly, taking pictures.

3

It wasn't cold out or anything. Just a little cool. A brisk fall dusk. People lingering around the park. Others walking through. I moved on to Sixth Avenue and the basketball courts. Kids with fingers latched in chainlinks, waiting for a game. I wandered past the derelicts in the subway station, then back to the square, and sat against a wall near a guy in a wheelchair. He wore a green cap and had gray hair sticking out. A sign hung on one of the wheels read: DIABETIC

HOMELESS. The top of the sign had two holes with masking-tape grommets and was looped to the wheel by gray shoestring. The guy shook his can at people going by. After a minute he turned on me, annoyed.

"Whatta you want?" he said.

"Nothing."

"Well, you're sittin there staring—it's buggin me." He shook his can again. "It's gotta be somethin. What is it?"

"I want a picture."

"Aw fuck," he said. "A picture of the cripple."

"It's not like that."

"The fuckin cripple," he said.

"I take pictures of everyone. It's not a big deal," I said.

"Gimme a dollar."

I gave him a dollar. He looked at the bill, surprised, then shoved it in his can. His attitude switched from annoyance to imperiousness. He took an old plastic bottle from a cotton sack that closed with a red drawstring. A mouthful of water sloshed at the bottom of the bottle.

"Fill this," he demanded.

There was a water fountain across the street, but it had been turned off for the winter. I walked over to the bathroom at the south end of the park and rinsed the lid, which was crusted with yellowish debris. I filled the bottle with cold water, then brought it back. Without looking at it he stuck the bottle between his legs.

"So what you waitin for?" he said.

"You sure?"

"Kid asks am I sure."

I began taking photographs. At first he looked stern. Then

he smiled in a blissful, phony way, making fun of me. Then he turned to the side, sick of it, and that was the shot I wanted. When I finished I sat and rewound the film. He pretended to ignore me, but he wasn't angry anymore. He seemed interested.

"So what else?" he said.

"What do you mean what else?"

"You're still sittin there. You want something else."

"Can I ask a question?"

"Oh, now there's questions."

"To write beneath the picture. To say who you are."

"I'm Stump. Call me Stump."

"Stump."

"That's what they call me. At the shelter," he added.

"That's not too nice."

"Yeah, well, you ever been in the shelter?"

I went on and asked which shelter and how old he was and how long he'd been there and why he was in a wheelchair and he answered each question brusquely. I asked him what he did with his free time and he looked at me.

"I mean besides this."

He just looked away. I could see he'd had enough of me.

"I'll bring you a copy," I said.

"I don't give a fuck."

I put my notebook in my back pocket and shook his hand. As I left he yelled, "You sell that, you make any money off that, you bring me somethin."

I took a last shot of him against the wall. Then I kept walking.

4

I peered through the little square window. They were all hunched together in the blue surgical scrubs, heads down, hands working. A nurse saw me and one of the men in scrubs turned. He had a mask on but I could tell it was Norman. He motioned with his eyes, and I left the window, walked back down, and waited in the courtyard. Twenty minutes later he came out in just the scrubs, arms bare, pretending he wasn't cold. He was a big guy, with an authoritarian air. The most ordinary sentences came out with a tone of accusation. Basically, he looked like a thug, and had a grating, unpleasant personality.

"I haven't seen you," he said, leaning against the bench.

"I'm right across the street. I haven't seen you, either."

There were three nurses at a picnic table in the corner—I watched them talking with one another, laughing.

"So you got it?" I asked.

"I wouldn't've bothered coming if I didn't."

He placed a roll of film on the table. When he was younger he'd gotten in a lot of fights. He didn't yell or make threats when he was angry, but his posture stiffened, and you could see the muscle on the side of his face near his jaw. An aggressive lowering of the head. The three nurses stood, cleaning their table. One of them looked at Norman, then looked away quickly. I could tell she did not like him.

"You been sleeping?" he said.

"Yeah yeah."

"Cause you look like shit," he said, and I just took the canister off the table and turned it over in my fingers. The expiration date was October 3, 1987. It had been three years.

"Don't freak out," Norman said.

"Who's the one freaking out?"

"Gotta be me," he said, and I didn't say anything to that. I put the canister in my pocket, and he stepped from the table.

"I only had a minute," he said.

Without shaking my hand he went back inside, and I sat there watching an older guy with a facial droop fumbling with the door. He tried to get the latch three or four times and then finally he lurched out, dragging the right foot. I took a shot of him, of his reflection in the dark glass, and then of birds going by in the reflection, crossing him. I put my camera away and went downstairs and locked myself in a bathroom. I turned off all the lights and sat on the tiles against the cool, porcelain wall. I felt better there, hidden in the dark. The eerie underground sounds of the hospital amplified, multiplied, overlapped, and I sat in the dark, very quiet and still, listening. After fifteen minutes I let myself out, walked to the locker room, and changed into my work clothes. It was exactly five o'clock.

5

Gil Hock, slender, unshaven, and pigeon-toed, with a wide nose and a little brown mustache, stood in the hospital loading bay in his Station Eighteen medic jacket, holding the photograph of the dead kid into the fading light. He studied the print, and then returned it with a sort of deprecation.

"You got a sick talent. You know that, Frank?"

I slid the photograph into my pocket.

"You oughtta take pictures of healthy people."

"I don't like healthy people."

"Like I said," he murmured. "A sick talent." He cleared his throat, crooked his head to the side, spit. "Who was he?"

"Some HIV kid."

"Full-blown?"

"Yeah."

"Just decided . . ."

He put a finger to his head. I nodded.

"Smart kid," he said. Then, "You got anything else?"

"That's it."

"Well," he said in a softer tone. "It's enough. Has Classon seen these?"

"I don't know if he needs to," I said, and he nodded. He'd been looking up and down the block the whole time, waiting for someone. "What's today's special?" I asked.

Hock opened his palm, revealing five cylindrical glass vials with tapered ends, each filled with a yellowish liquid.

"Meatloaf," he said, and that was all he said. I could see it was liquid Valium.

Across the street Burnett, my partner, came out of a run-down-looking four-story redbrick building. This was the old nurse's residence, condemned now, but a corner of it supposedly had been cleaned up and was used by EMS. Burnett stood on the concrete stoop, hands on his hips. A big guy, with weightlifter's arms, a goatee, and bushy brown eyebrows. He wasn't the smartest person at the station, and so he made up for it by being abrasive, loud, a showoff. He yowled my name across the street, gesturing impatiently, then stepped out to meet me, glancing resentfully at the slight figure of Gil Hock.

"Why you always gotta be talkin to him? What the fuck did he want?"

6

Four o'clock in the afternoon in Washington Square Park. I'd gotten Emily Pascal's phone number from the hospital records, called her, and now, in the slanting afternoon light, Emily and a friend of hers, Myra, looked at my photographs, which I'd set out on the rounded edge of the dry fountain.

"You can see where I fell. The cut jeans. Everything. There's where the bullet came through. He's just on the other side of the door."

"He should've been more careful," Myra said. "He wants to hurt himself, big deal. But he should be careful about someone else."

Emily straightened the photographs on the edge of the fountain.

"Can I see it?" I pointed at her leg.

"It's not pretty."

"Like he's not used to it," Myra said.

Emily sat on the edge of the fountain and I raised her pants leg to reveal a loose five-by-ten dressing. I touched it.

"Does that hurt?"

"I feel it," she said.

The skin was reddish beneath the gauze, bulging at the black seams. Myra stepped to the side to watch. I did not have gloves on, and as I reached in to peel the bandage back further, Myra said, "I wouldn't touch it."

"I'm not touching it."

"She—"

"I'm not touching it."

I brought my camera out and took a medium shot of the wound. A close-up with the stitched flesh crossing the frame at an angle. A shot from the side, showing the extent of the bruises. A long shot with Emily looking directly, blankly, into the camera, her left leg out straight and the curved edge of the fountain in the background with dried leaves blown up against the wall. Myra smiled as the camera turned on her, and stopped smiling as soon as it left. Bandaging Emily's leg with fresh gauze, I said, "You could make some money off this."

"A lawsuit?" Myra guessed.

"Yes."

She looked knowingly at Emily. They must have spoken of it earlier.

"He didn't have any money," Emily said.

"The city does," I said. "The city's the landlord on that building. The door's supposed to be sealed. And the cops arrived with their sirens. That's against protocol for a suicidal patient. They could be held liable."

"And you must know a lawyer or something," Myra said.

"Yeah, sure," I said.

Again, Myra looked at Emily.

"If you use the lawyer I get a commission. If you want to use your own lawyer you can still have the pictures. If you win you can give me something."

"How much could she make?" Myra asked.

"Two hundred thousand," I said.

"Oh come on," Emily said.

I shrugged.

"You were shot. Two hundred thousand dollars isn't a lot for being shot." I finished bandaging her leg and rolled the pants leg down. "I'm not saying you have to do it. I'm just saying check it out. Talk to someone."

I could see Myra agreed. Emily studied the top photograph.

"It'd take a long time," Emily said.

"If you settled out of court it'd be quick. Two, three months. You'd make less."

"How much less?" Myra asked.

"A hundred thousand."

I was making the numbers up. Myra smiled at Emily, who dropped her head.

"I'm gonna take a walk," Emily said. "I'm gonna walk to the fountain and think about it. You can wait."

Emily straightened her jeans and started toward the drinking fountain. I knew that fountain barely worked, but I let her go. She needed time to think. The other girl, Myra, was left standing alone with me.

"If it was me who got shot, I'd look into it," Myra said. "I mean, why not? Free money. But she doesn't care. She'll just decide based on some whim, based on how she feels walking to the drinking fountain. I bet she says no."

A resentful tone in Myra's voice. Far away, Emily tried the fountain, then, tilting her head, opened her mouth on the place where the water burbled weakly from the rusty nozzle. Myra and Emily both had large navy-blue canvas bags. Myra saw me looking at them.

"Fencing," she said. "We fence."

I thought she meant something else, but then she unzipped her bag and took out a silver foil. Held it out.

"Fencing," she said again. "We're competitors."

She bounced forward on her toes, jabbing with the foil, then bounced back. An agile, athletic motion. Fencing. She lowered the foil slowly. Five-four, a lithe way of moving, short, straight blond hair—I thought she was pretty. She saw me looking at her and lowered her eyes. I figured I had nothing to lose.

"Do you have a boyfriend?" I asked. The end of her foil wavered over the pavement. "I'm not saying I . . . know you or anything. You seem nice. The sort of person I like. I thought I could call you."

She scrunched her face and looked away. She seemed surprised, though maybe not in a bad way.

She said, "Come to the club."

I didn't understand.

"We're going to the club. To work out. You can watch."

"All right."

"You want to?"

"Uhm, yeah. That'd be great. To the club."

Emily was walking back slowly. Myra frowned at her.

"You shouldn't touch your mouth to the fountain. I wouldn't want to drink after that."

"Yeah yeah. You're right."

"I mean, that's pretty rude."

Emily lowered her eyes.

"Did you decide?" I asked her.

"I can't do it."

"Aw."

"It's not against you or anything. It's probably a good idea. Myra thinks so. I just . . . I'm not wasting time in court, with lawyers."

"You could make a lot of money," Myra said.

"I'm not doing it," Emily said in a firm tone that surprised me. Afterward, there was a moment of silence, all of us looking down.

"He's coming to the club," Myra said. "I invited him."

The two friends exchanged looks.

7

Hock and Burnett were in the loading bay across the street from the station. All the supplies for the sixteen-floor hospital were brought in at these bays, and all the trash taken out from there, too. It was an ugly area of parked trucks, diesel fumes, oily black concrete, enormous Dumpsters, six-foot exhaust fans, and a dull green hose that leaked steaming gray water twenty-four hours a day. Hock liked to talk back there—with the idling of the trucks and the roar from the exhaust fans, he could not be overheard. I knew Burnett would ask about Emily. He was counting on the money. As I walked up, Hock said, "You don't look happy." Then to Burnett. "He look happy to you?"

"Nah, he don't," Burnett said. Then, "So what happened, Frank?"

I put my hands in my pockets.

"She wasn't interested. Thinks it's a waste of time."

"She could've made a lot of fuckin money."

"She doesn't care."

"How can she not care?"

"She's got HIV."

"What the fuck's that supposed to mean?"

"It means she thinks she doesn't have a lot of time to mess around in. And she figures it's the city. You know how slow the city is. By the time that money comes through she'll be dead."

"She's got a point there," Hock said, gesturing with a cigarette.

"What else she gonna do?" Burnett asked.

"She fences."

"What?"

"She fences. With swords."

"It's a kind of sport," Hock said to Burnett. "Like you see on TV."

He was baiting Burnett.

"And that's why she didn't wanna file?"

"That's why."

"Aw fuck."

Hock looked straight ahead. Burnett's histrionics bored him.

"I got a kid on the way," Burnett said.

Hock tapped Burnett with the back of his hand.

"Would you quit it about your kid?"

"I'm just sayin."

"I know you're just sayin. You've been just sayin it about fifty times." Then, to me, "He's been sayin it all day."

Hock was five inches shorter and sixty pounds lighter than Burnett, but Burnett deferred to him. Hock was a station leader, a guy people looked up to, went to for advice. Burnett was seen as a sort of clown.

"You tried to convince her?" Burnett asked. "You showed her the pictures?"

"She liked those."

"Glad to hear it. Glad she got something out of it. You tell her those pictures were worth money? A lotta fuckin money?"

"She didn't care."

"What I heard is she's some college-looking girl. Doesn't need money. Like Frank."

"Yeah. Like me."

"Ah fuck," Burnett said again. "You at least get her number?"

"I got it. But she doesn't want to be bothered."

"Bothered by what?"

"Someone calling, I guess."

"I don't see how that's a bother. How is that a fuckin bother?"

"I don't know."

"Explain it to me, Frank."

"I don't know," I said again. "All I know is that she didn't want anyone calling. She seemed pretty adamant about it."

Burnett looked confused.

"It means she won't do it," Hock said to Burnett, and Burnett said, "I don't need you to fuckin translate. I know what it means. I'm disappointed. I could use the money."

"Yeah yeah. We know. For the kid."

"That's right. For the fuckin kid."

I crossed my arms. Leaned on my heels.

"I called her friend, though."

"What?"

"She came with a friend. I asked her friend out."

"Jesus."

"Frank's supposed to be selling her on the idea of filing a suit, and what's he doing? He's askin her fuckin friend out. Her friend have HIV, too?"

"I hope not."

Burnett turned to Hock.

"Whatta you think, Gil?"

"I think he should wear a condom," Hock said.

I just stood there, letting Burnett cool down bit by bit.

8

I snapped the film from its casing and set the spool in the developing tank and screwed the top so it was sealed. I did that all by feel, in the dark. I poured the developer in and swirled the canister, and then worked my way along the bench and turned on the safelight. There was a kind of comfort in its weightless, red glow. I looked at my watch. I had an hour.

The darkroom was a converted storage space in my apartment with a wooden bench at one end and a narrow cot at the other. The enlarger rested on the bench, and, alongside that, several bins for the developing fluid, the stop, the fixer, the wash. There was a higher shelf where I kept extra chemicals, and a thin cord at eye level with wooden safety pins in a plastic bin nearby for clipping photographs. There was a drying rack in the far corner and a large corkboard with many photographs pinned to it, some notes written with a black marker directly on the prints. Beneath the bench there was a little shelf holding photography books and paperback novels. Alongside that, a box of quarter-molding from which I made frames. I'd stored bottled water beneath the bed and some nuts and raisins in a cylindrical jar up on the high shelf. I even had a urinal from the hospital in case I wanted to go and couldn't open the door. Everything I needed to survive in there for hours, even days.

I checked my watch, sat back, and waited. I should have

used that time to get dressed but I didn't. When the timer sounded I poured out the developer, poured in the stop, and after that the fixer. I unscrewed the top from the developing tank, held the negatives to the light, dried them with a blow-dryer, then made a contact sheet, which had a one-inch image from every negative. The first shot showed a man in his mid-forties wearing jeans with frayed cuffs and a collared shirt. He was sitting on the floor, leaning forward, a sandwich on a napkin to his left, and on the right, above, a potted plant and an ashtray on a windowsill. I didn't like the composition of this picture at all. I thought I'd stood too close. That it was slightly underexposed. That the subject was self-conscious, stiff, unrevealing. I found the print I'd developed a few days before, the one of the dead kid against the painted door. I lay it alongside the contact sheet, comparing the two. Looking at that second print, I was jolted to attention. It was like seeing the kid for the first time. Tiny hole in his forehead. Large, grotesque splash behind him. Blank eyes. I saw all of this with a clarity and precision that I did not have when I was in the room. It struck me with more force than the actual event but without some of the horror. That first shot of the man with the sandwich was worthless. I felt nothing looking at it other than impatience and disappointment that I was the one who'd taken the photograph and embarrassment that someone else might see it. That was all.

When the contact sheet was only half dry I cut out the first photograph, the one of the sitting man, folded it, and slid it into my pocket. I figured at some point, like it or not,

Norman would want to see it. I hurried into the main room. Framed and unframed photographs covered the walls. There were prints stacked on all the exposed surfaces, and photography books at the head of a futon on the floor. Negatives were pinned to a corkboard on the north wall. An old enlarger rested beneath a winter jacket. I ought to have hurried, but I didn't. I just stood there. Then I turned and went back inside the darkroom and shut the door and sat against the wall with the muffled city sounds filtering in and the safelight glowing. I glanced at the contact sheet again, looked away quickly, and then I was crying. It came on me all at once, catching me unexpectedly. I felt ashamed but I couldn't help it. I was crying. After fifteen minutes or so, my breathing slowed. I wiped my eyes and looked at my watch and said something like, Oh fuck. I was very late. I thought of not going at all. But then I thought, What's the use of not going? What worse thing can happen?

I left without even looking in the mirror.

9

Through the doorway of Sidewalk, a restaurant in the East Village, I saw Myra, at the bar, reading a psychology textbook. She'd gone past the point of looking up when the door opened, and I could tell she was angry. Of course she was angry. I was more than an hour late. Any normal person would have been angry about that. I made an excuse about the subway, about the rain, but she wasn't interested in my excuses. She'd decided I was a fuckup. There was an empty glass in front of her. I tried to order her another drink and she hesitated, almost said no, then said o.k., she'd have one more. I ordered a drink, too.

"I have a picture of you."

In the photograph, taken at the club, she was leaning against the wall, exhausted after her workout, looking over her shoulder at the camera. I rarely took pictures of healthy people, and definitely not of people I knew, so I was interested to see how she'd react. She took the print, only glanced at it, and said, "I'm not smiling."

"No."

She made a little sniffing noise, then put the photograph in her purse.

"It would look better if I was smiling," she said.

I asked about the fencing, and her graduate school in psychology, her home in Pennsylvania. She answered tersely, not making it easy for me. I had to talk the whole time. A half-hour passed, and, having nothing left to talk about, I said, "I have another picture," and tossed it on the bar. The print was still wet when I'd put it in my pocket and the edges had stuck together. I had to rip it a little to get them apart.

"My father," I said.

Myra looked closely. The lighting in the photograph made him look very young.

"How old is he?" she said.

"He would be forty-nine."

Her face changed, and I told her how he died, and how he did it.

She didn't say anything to that. I took the photograph from her, folded it carefully, and put it in my pocket. I could see she felt uncomfortable. It was a stupid thing to bring up. A minute later she stood. I called for the tab. The bartender brought it over, looked between us, then gave it to me. It was for twenty-five dollars. We'd had two drinks.

"You were late," she said. "I had a drink before you came."

"Ah . . . good," I said.

"I saw a friend. He had a drink, too."

"Whatever."

I left thirty dollars. She looked to see what I'd put down and when she saw I'd left a good tip she softened a little. We walked out together. We were on Avenue A. She lived a few blocks from there. I carried her bag. When we got to her stoop I set the bag on the ground, and she said, "I live right here, on the first floor." I waited while she unlocked the front door, and I was surprised when she held the door for me. We walked down the hallway silently. She opened her apartment door. We went inside. It was a small one-bedroom. She had two stuffed animals on the couch, a poster of Italy, another of a tiger, a framed photograph of a group of girls all smiling and holding plastic cups. I set the bag down inside the doorway and she pushed the door shut but did not close it all the way. I said it was nice meeting her, so she wouldn't get scared or think I misunderstood her. Then she faced me, head tilted up. I didn't hesitate. I kissed her. She kept her head up. I tried to kiss her again and I thought she wanted me to but at the last moment she pulled away and put a hand over her mouth and stepped to a mirror, looking in it closely, as if I'd hurt her. She rubbed a finger on her upper lip.

"I think I have a pimple starting," she said.

I apologized about being late. She studied her lip in the mirror. I said good-bye, then walked down the hallway slowly, thinking maybe she'd open the door and say good-bye or give me a call or something like that. She didn't. I paused at the stairs, then went down to the street. The entire date had taken about forty minutes. I walked into Tompkins Square. It had rained earlier and the benches were wet. Beads of water reflecting streetlights. I tried to wipe one of the benches off with my hand but it didn't work. I just sat in the water. A while later I lay with my feet up and the dark branches overhead, the sound of horns, car wheels on wet pavement. A homeless guy with a grocery bag sat on a bench nearby and put his head in his hands. He began shaking. He looked like he could have been laughing or talking to himself but I knew he wasn't. I got up and walked past him slowly, thinking maybe I'd take a photograph of him. He didn't even look up. I took a shot from down the sidewalk and went on toward my apartment.

10

Broken plasterboard, old tiles, and long, fragile, fluorescent lights lay in a heap near the Dumpsters behind the hospital. Burnett drew one of the glass tubes from the trash and flung it carelessly against the brick wall. It was after work and we were all a little drunk. Down 136th Street, near the doctors' parking lot, I saw Norman. He had a distinctive walk—an energetic, bobbing strut, arms out to the side—and he always wore these snakeskin cowboy boots that he'd gotten in Laredo. It was embarrassing, really, the way he wore them all the time. I stepped behind the Dumpsters and bent on one knee, tying my boot. I undid one lace and tied it up slowly. As I was doing the other boot I heard Hock say, "Hey, Doc."

"Hey."

"Where's Frank?" Burnett said.

"Haven't seen'm," Norman said. He went on to the hospital.

I finished with my laces and walked back around the piled trash. Burnett was holding a glass tube. Hock stood with his thumbs hooked in the waist of his jeans.

"Hey, Frank. Your brother came by," he said, and Burnett and Hock looked at each other, laughing.

"What's the deal with the boots?" Burnett said.

"He's going to save the town," I said. "He's the hero."

Hock made a shooting motion with his finger. Burnett mimicked his walk, and then held out the fluorescent light. Cool, smooth, fragile glass in my palm. Burnett nodded to the wall.

11

Four bullet holes in the wire-mesh glass, the lobby's long, high window filled with blue light, and a circular plate in the ceiling where there'd once been a chandelier. All of it abandoned, boarded-up, the marble tiled floor rough with plaster grit. A few mattresses against the wall on the east side, and everywhere old bottles, cigarette butts, paper garbage, discarded lighters, needles, pipes. The air hot, stifling, and the muffled roar from a fire. We could hear soft cracks and moans overhead.

"Hey, look't this," Burnett shouted, holding something up. We were rifling through debris in the lobby. "A bayonet."

"A what?"

"A knife, a bayonet." He waved it around, then wedged it, blade-down, on his right side, beneath the belt. "We just find that rifle we'll be in business."

He was kicking through some soiled blankets, using a flashlight to turn them over so he did not have to touch them. Suddenly he stopped and was quiet.

"What?"

"Shh . . ."

And then I heard it, too.

"Help, help!" a voice cried above us, and Burnett turned to me, smiling.

"Gimme a fuckin break," he said. "I can't believe it."

We found him on the third-floor hallway. He was a sixty-year-old black guy who'd fallen through the rotten floorboards and broken his ankle. He was trapped. The split planks bowed inward so it squeezed when he tried to pull out. The sound from the fire was much louder up there, the heat was incredible, and the paint overhead was beginning to bubble and flake off like a time-lapse movie.

"Take a picture, Frank."

Burnett bent to the guy and put two hands lightly on his lower leg, and I took a picture. I took a close-up of the deformed part of the leg, and then I lay on the floor with the guy to the side in the foreground, the glow from the fire and the bubbled ceiling overhead.

"Not to tell you your business, but this ain't the time for snapshots," the guy said.

"This ain't the time for snapshots," Burnett said. "You hear that?" Then, impatiently, "Documentation. It's for documentation."

A moment later Burnett lifted the guy beneath the arms, and while he was supporting him, I reached my hand in the hole, broke the pieces of wood off, and his leg came free. He didn't cry out, but only caught his breath a few times, and let out a sigh of relief as Burnett set him into our folding chair. Burnett nodded up to the fourth floor, and said, "Go on, Frank. Why not?"

In the stairway I could feel the heat reflecting off the walls. The air shimmered. The fourth floor came into view and it was suddenly even hotter, flames all up and down the walls, buckling and cracking the floorboards, and the sound deafening, like a train. I got an angle shot of the hallway, and afterward, for a moment, I just stood there, practically surrounded by flames. Then I came running down. My clothes were steaming.

"I think you're on fire," Burnett said.

He'd already taken a blanket and tape and wrapped the guy's leg up in a makeshift splint. I took a shot of that, and a minute later we were carrying him out the front door.

We'd heard the fire trucks arrive. The firemen were tearing out the plywood from the buildings on either side, hacking into walls with sledgehammers and axes. The people from the block came out and watched offhandedly, as if it were a completely normal and ordinary thing. And it was, really. In the late eighties Harlem lost a third of its population—whole neighborhoods where absentee landlords defaulted on their taxes and turned the property over to the city, or lit a match and collected on the insurance. That sort of thing happened every day.

"This used to be a nice block," the old guy said as we lifted him into the ambulance. "Wouldn't know it now, but it was a nice block."

"What're you complaining about?" Burnett said. "Downtown looks nice, don't it? And it's gonna trickle down."

Burnett walked up front. We could hear him laughing to himself as he got into the driver's seat. Twenty minutes later, as we were leaving the ER, an EMS lieutenant walked toward us. I turned away and bent for the drinking fountain. It was against protocol for us to go into burning buildings. It was practically the first thing they taught us. I thought he'd stick it to us, but lieutenants, in general, were pretty slack. The city was falling apart. We were at ground zero in the worst wave of violence of the century. As long as we didn't fuck up completely we were pretty much left alone.

"What the hell is that?" I heard the lieutenant say, and turned to see him pulling the bayonet from Burnett's belt, winging it around in the ER. Burnett snatched it from him, and gave the lieutenant a contemptuous look. "Necessary implement for access and egress. Gimme a break."

Back in the ambulance, Burnett tossed the wide, beveled blade on the dashboard.

"Whatta you think? It's gotta be worth somethin, right?"

12

Three brothers played along the iron fence in a subsidized-housing project in Chelsea. The two older boys tried to slip their heads through the fence, but the bars were too narrowly spaced. The youngest brother crammed his head between the bars. The older boys tried to get him to go all the way through, but he jerked his head back and they all laughed. Their grandmother sat on a bench, smoking cigarettes, holding a rottweiler on a leash that she'd looped to the back of the bench. Overweight, jaundiced, sullen, smoking the whole time, she dropped the butts between the wooden planks. I wanted a photograph of her but it seemed unnatural always to fixate on that sort of thing. I took a few shots of the kids playing at the fence and then I took a shot of the three of them in a line with the fence stretching away at an angle in the background. Then of each individually. In every photograph the kids were happy, smiling. Just as I was leaving I took a furtive shot of the grandmother, then went on to my apartment and developed the film into a contact sheet. I looked at the images through the developing fluid and afterward held them up to the safelight. I went out and bought some beer and drank one of them on the way back. I went into the darkroom and looked at the prints of the children again. I opened another beer and set it on top of the contact sheet. A while later I reached over and tossed the sheet in the garbage and went on drinking.

13

We found Rolly reclined on sloped concrete rubble in the courtyard of an abandoned building. His legs out, ankles as thick as his thighs, his hand fished for a bottle wedged between two bricks.

"I wanna go to hospital oh-seven," he said. "I'm sick."

He wasn't sick. Rolly called every day. He got drunk every day, needed a place to stay, so he called us to take him to the hospital, where he slept on a stretcher that they'd wheel out into a hallway near the lobby.

I set the drug bag in the dirt. Burnett found a red milk crate, brushed dust from the top, sat, and tapped Rolly's bottle with the antenna of his radio.

"What're you drinking?"

"Thunderbird."

"How much was it?"

"Two oh nine."

Burnett turned, smiling.

"Two oh nine. He knows it exactly. That with or without tax?"

"With tax. Dollar ninety-four without."

"Jesus."

"Dollar ninety-four warm. Dollar ninety-nine cold."

Burnett gave me a look.

"Guy's a whiz with numbers. How much's Night Train?"

"Dollar eighty-seven with tax. Dollar seventy-five without."

"And warm?"

"I already told you. Nickel less. Dollar seventy."

"Whattaya buy it? Warm or cold?"

Rolly rolled his shoulders.

"Don't matter to me. Warm or cold. I won't lie to you. I just wanna drink." He looked over as if he recognized me for the first time. "Take a picture," he said.

"He remembers you take pictures."

"I don't need a picture," I said. "I got ten of you sitting right there. Do something new and I'll take a picture of that. Like if you were sober. That'd be a picture."

"Aw."

"What?"

"You're mad," he said. "You in a bad mood today."

Burnett placed two fingers on Rolly's knee.

"You ever had a job?"

"Sure I had a job."

"What?"

"I boxed."

"You boxed?"

"Look at his hands," I said.

Burnett rolled a concrete lump the size of a baseball in his fingers. He looked at Rolly critically.

"So where'd you box?"

"All over. Vegas. Wherever."

"What happened?"

"Nothing happened."

"Why didn't you stay in the boxing business?"

"I guess I had enough."

"You started drinking. That's what happened," Burnett said.

"I was sent to prison is what happened."

"Bullshit."

"All right."

"What for?"

"Killing someone."

"Bullshit," Burnett said again. He cleared his throat and spit past Rolly's foot. "You listenin to this?" he said to me.

"What else would I be doing?"

"Guy was messing with me," Rolly said. "Messing with my woman."

"Uh-huh," Burnett said. "What'd you use to kill him? Gun?"

"I didn't use anything," he said. "I used myself."

"Look at his hands," I said again.

Rolly had enormous, knobby, arthritic hands. Old boxer's hands. He could not close them all the way.

"So how long'd you do?"

"Six years eight months. Parole for two."

"And where'd you do it?"

"Couple places."

"Where was the first?"

"Attica."

"What'd you do there?"

"Worked in the kitchen. Did that two years."

"What cell block?"

"Eight."

"You were in cell block eight?"

"That's what I just said."

"And after that?"

"I was down in four."

"What'd you do there?"

"Still in the kitchen."

"And how long for that?"

"Nine months. Then I was upstate. Sing Sing. In two north. I made street signs."

The three other buildings that formed the courtyard were all abandoned and boarded, here and there a window showing black where the plywood had fallen or been pried off for some other use. Pigeons sat on concrete window ledges.

"What'd you do when you got out?" Burnett asked.

"I didn't do anything," he said.

"You didn't go back into the boxing business?"

"No."

"And the woman?"

Rolly just looked away and didn't answer. Burnett tossed his lump of concrete aside and stood.

"Get up, Rolly."

Rolly reached for his green bottle. Burnett pushed his hand away.

"Nah. You're not drinking anymore. Get up."

Burnett held Rolly at arm's length.

"You boxed?"

"I don't anymore," Rolly said.

"Of course you don't. You're an alcoholic. You're forty-two and can hardly walk. Your ankles're like a fucking elephant's. And every day you're calling. Bugging us. Forget that we could be helping someone else. I could be eating my lunch."

Burnett held him by the shoulder. I noticed a kid watching from around the corner of the building.

"Jack," I said.

Burnett saw the kid, and glowered. The kid ducked away. I stepped over to check the slot between the two buildings. The kid had stopped halfway. When he saw me he kept on running and tailed off onto the sidewalk, out of sight. Burnett turned back.

"Show me how you used to box, Rolly."

"I don't do it no more," he said in a meek voice.

"Show me how you used to."

Rolly raised his hands to his chest and Burnett punched him in the jaw, grabbing Rolly's collar to keep him from falling. Burnett punched him again so I heard the clacking sound as Rolly's teeth knocked against each other. I started forward as if I was going to stop him. Then I turned as if to wait between the buildings. I could hear Burnett grunting behind me, the sound of flesh on flesh. I turned again. I brought my camera out and took a shot of Burnett hitting. Burnett smacking with his open hand. Burnett pushing him back when Rolly tried to protect himself. Burnett smiling with his arm around Rolly's neck. Burnett prodding him on with one stiff arm between the shoulderblades.

"I gotta wear gloves. He almost fucking bled on me."

14

The ambulance was parked twenty yards down the block to the left. To our right was a concrete stoop. The boy I'd seen before stood on the other side of the stoop, and was talking to a man and woman through the bars of the railing. When we came out from between the two buildings they all looked up and the boy walked away quickly, glancing over his shoulder several times. The woman, tall, skinny, with bony knees and elbows, yelled out, "You all right, Rolly?"

"Yeah, I'm all right," he yelled back.

"You're bleeding!" she shrieked. She stood abruptly. She was five foot nine, with big feet, and big hands, and an inch of matted hair. She was about forty years old. She tapped the man sitting beside her. "He's bleeding!"

"I'm all right," Rolly said over his shoulder.

A raised edge to the sidewalk, and as Rolly looked back his foot caught the edge. Burnett supported him with one hand under his left arm. Rolly leaned on Burnett, then slumped and sat on the pavement. Burnett stood over him, smiling.

"Get up, Rolly," Burnett said.

"He's bleeding!" the woman down the block shrieked again. "Look't'm! Look't his face! He's bleeding! They hurt him!"

"I don't fucking believe this," Burnett muttered. Then yelling to the woman, "He fell down. He's drunk."

"His mouth's bleeding! I see it! Blood!"

The woman stood. The man stood, too, reluctantly. He was a trim-looking guy wearing khakis, a white button-down shirt, and a gold chain with a gold cross around his neck. Fifty years old. Some church guy. The two walked over, the scrawny lady striding quickly, waving an arm, and the short, well-dressed man following behind.

"He's not bleeding," Burnett said.

"He's bleeding!"

"That's wine," Burnett said. Then to me, "Talk to her, Frank."

"He was drinking when we found him. That red you see is wine."

"That ain't wine."

"Night Train."

"Lie!" she screamed. "Lie! Lie!"

The left side of her mouth twitched. She squinched her eyes shut and stood with her head turned, shaking. An older woman and two teenaged boys approached, wheeling one of those wire carts that you tilt to push. She set the basket upright. Rolly sat on the concrete, looking drunk, bewildered. Burnett caught my eye.

"Get'm in the bus."

The trim little man bent to help.

"How you doin, Rolly?" the man asked in a gentle voice, and Burnett, who was already annoyed by the gathering crowd, said impatiently, "We got him. Step back."

The man ignored him. Again, in a soft voice, "You hurt?"

Burnett held the man back with one hand. The woman with the grocery cart shouted, "Don't you touch him! He ain't done nothin! Don't you touch him!" Burnett made a little huffing noise and pushed the man back. He tried to raise Rolly with one hand but only dragged him across the concrete. Both women yelled out, "You're hurting him!"

"We're gettin him in the ambulance," Burnett said.

"He's bleedin!"

Burnett turned on me.

"You gonna help, Frank?"

I'd been standing back, fingering the camera in my pocket, wondering how to get a photograph without making a scene. As I stepped up, Burnett looked past me and his eyes grew wide, startled. I turned to see a flash of metal. Something passed under my right arm. I fell. A blossoming on my right side, a warmth that flowed into my entire body. There'd been an insulated feeling to the whole exchange, and then suddenly it was like that moment when you come out of an air-conditioned house into the heat of the day. I lost perhaps ten seconds. Then I was on my back with a view of sky between brownstones. I heard sirens faintly. People ran back and forth near my head, shouting. I lay there, overcome, for a moment, with a feeling of well-being. Burnett stood near my head, a blue glove on his right hand, pulling a glove on the left, saying, "I gotta protect myself, Frank, never know who you been fucking." I tried to sit up and was surprised when I couldn't. I tried to sit up again and Burnett held me down with two gloved fingers. They were putting me on a board. Strapping me in. I felt hands on either side of my head. Burnett placed three fingers on my wrist. "Frank," I heard someone say. "How you doin, Frank?" Burnett seemed far away. He was counting my pulse.

"I got one?" I asked.

He didn't answer.

"What is it?"

He stopped counting.

"Little fast."

"Burnett."

"Yeah."

"What is it?"

"One ten."

"How's it feel?"

"Like you'll live."

I was being lifted. Burnett had his gloved hand at my right side.

"How's that feel? That hurt?"

"Ah fuck."

"That?"

"Would you fucking stop it?"

We were in the ambulance. Burnett was bandaging me. I felt something both sharp and heavy on my side. I began to sit up and Burnett held me down.

"She get you anywhere else?"

"I don't know."

I was lying on the stretcher looking up at the hanging bags of saline. Burnett was holding me down.

"How deep is it?" I asked.

"Hardly a scratch," he said.

"What was it?"

"Knife, Frank. Didn't you see it?"

I tried to sit up again. I was restless. "Come on, Frank. Jesus . . ." They put an oxygen mask on me. Burnett was saying, "Take it, easy, Frank. Fucking take it easy." I was infinitely grateful that it was Burnett treating me. He was a great medic. Much better than I was. He was a thug, but he was a great medic. Burnett was going into my arms with the needles, the clear lines swinging on either side. He was talking to the driver up front. Then we were at the hospital and they jerked me out. The wheels landed roughly, with a pain that jolted through my entire right side. I did not really feel it for a moment, and then I did.

Inside the trauma room, Towers and Joseph came into view over my head. There were two stethoscopes on my chest. They cut my uniform off. Six pairs of hands rolled me, and they felt my whole back, the area inside my legs, my neck, my stomach, my back again, a finger in my rectum. Dr. Towers was over me, listening with his stethoscope, and then taking it off one ear, then the other, smiling, and saying, "You must've said your prayers this week, Frank. Been a good boy." They gave me a chest tube and took a chest X-ray and gave me a unit of blood and listened to my lungs about eight times. Then they sent me upstairs where, later that night, Norman came in wearing surgical scrubs, a blue hairnet, and around his neck, a dangling white mask.

15

"You gotta see me now," he said.

"I don't mind seeing you," I said.

He raised my arm gently and peeled the bandage back to reveal a yellowed oblong splotch with red along the middle.

The skin was sewn tightly around the tube and the tube went into a basin that was bubbling, creating suction to re-inflate my lung. Just beneath my armpit on either side of the tube there were three inches of neat stitches. Little nubs of number-two black thread above the rolled purplish skin.

"Who did this?"

"Towers," I said.

"Sewed it, too?"

"Yeah."

"Must like you. I'd've given you a scar to remember."

He lay the bandage back. It hurt as he pressed the tape. Norman saw me flinch. The painkillers were wearing off.

"Saw the scan. It came in laterally, caudal. An inch from the subclavian."

"Could've solved all your problems," I said, and Norman immediately stiffened. His voice got hard. "You know what they're saying downstairs?"

"Hero paramedic wounded in the line of duty?"

He was sitting alongside the bed. He draped his arm over the back of the chair.

"They're saying it was retaliation for patient abuse."

"Who?"

"Reporters."

"Downstairs?"

"Yes."

I started laughing.

"You're fuckin kidding me. Jesus. Don't let them up here."

"I didn't."

"Where'd it say that?"

"On the news. And there were reporters. It'll be in the papers."

"Jesus," I said, and started laughing again.

"Well, don't take it too hard, Frank."

"Yeah yeah," I said. "Just don't let them up here."

He said he wouldn't, and then he waited. He saw I was not going to explain myself. I could see he wanted to say more about it, to scold me or something, but I was lying there with a chest tube. It wasn't like we were going to get into it at that point. He shrugged and after a minute stood up.

"You want me to call anyone?"

"No."

"Anyone you want me to talk to?"

"No," I said. "Who'd want to know?"

He hesitated, then just nodded and walked out. I was left alone with the curtain pulled round me, the clamor from eight other patients snoring and moaning and calling Nurse Nurse Nurse I need help Nurse, the throbbing feeling in my side, and the faint sound of sirens and traffic that kept me company all night as I tried to sleep and could not.

16

It was the next afternoon. I was still in the ICU. I heard Burnett in the hallway.

"Where'd you hide my partner? Where the fuck's my partner?"

He strode up the aisle of beds, the nurses turning to see who was making all the noise.

"Frank!" he shouted.

I reached out to shake his hand. It hurt to move my arm. It hurt even to breathe. He looked at the chest tube.

"Got you hooked up. Jesus."

He asked about the wound, what they'd done, and when I'd get out. Then he pulled the knife from his pocket, folded it out from the handle halfway, and tossed it on the sheet over my legs.

"Souvenir," he said.

I opened the blade all the way and held it to the light.

"Who was she?"

"Some crackhead. They don't know her name. They ain't doin shit, Frank. They don't even have an address or nothin. They say she's homeless. Some—" He waved his hand. "Crackhead. I wouldn't be expectin nothing."

"I don't care," I said, which made Burnett laugh.

"You're one apathetic motherfucker," he said.

I could tell he thought this was a particularly ingratiating compliment. He leaned back, trying to be pleasant. I knew he'd come for a reason.

"You heard what they're sayin?"

"Yeah, I heard."

"Calling it retaliation for patient abuse."

"They can't prove it," I said.

"Well, the woman—"

"The grocery woman?"

Burnett spoke quietly.

"She filed a complaint."

I shrugged and rolled my eyes.

"Like that'll do anything. I'll say I don't know what the fuck she's talkin about. I'll say we were doing our job and we were attacked for no reason. You say the same thing. End of story."

Burnett seemed relieved. He'd acted like he didn't care, but I could see he'd been worried. He touched my knee through the sheet.

"You're all right, Frank. You're a dumbfuck, but for a college boy, you're all right." Then, looking over his shoulder, "You need anything?"

"Nah, I'm fine."

"If you need anything . . ."

I said I was fine. He looked at his watch, thanked me, and stood. I watched him strutting up the aisle, a roll to his walk that had not been there before. A moment later Emily Pascal walked in.

17

She was carrying that same blue duffel bag I'd seen before. I hadn't spoken with her since the day I'd met her in Washington Square Park and we'd all gone to the club.

"Hey," she said.

She placed the bag at the foot of the bed. She could tell I was surprised to see her.

"I was in the clinic. I saw it on the news."

"Ah."

"They said you were stabbed."

"Yeah. That's right."

She leaned over to see the tube coming out of my side.

"They got that going right up into you?"

"It bubbles down there," I pointed. "Makes a vacuum, a suction, that pulls the lung back out slowly. It takes a few days."

She seemed impressed—a tube going right into me. That was a big deal. I told her to look in the drawer of the bedside table. She took the knife out and opened it. Slashed it through the air. Then folded it back up. She looked to see if anyone was nearby.

"You heard the news?" she said.

She was the third person who'd asked me that.

"Yeah, I heard. It's bullshit," I said. "I didn't touch him."

"You didn't seem like the—"

"I didn't touch him."

"Maybe your partner, but not you. That's what I thought," she said.

I liked her for that.

"Did you talk to Myra?" I asked.

Her face changed a little.

"She said you never called her back. She said you were late for the date."

"That's true. I was."

"She hates it when people are late. She's a stickler about that. About a lot of things, but particularly about that. And then you didn't call her back."

"I figured there was no use. It didn't seem like she wanted me to call back. I figured . . . I might as well not."

"You should call her," Emily said woodenly. "You should come by the club."

"She doesn't want to see me."

"She will," Emily said.

"I doubt it."

"I'll talk to her," Emily said. "She wants to see you."

"Yeah?"

"I'll tell her it wasn't you who did anything. She'll like it that you were wrongly accused. That's exciting. I'll tell her all that. I'll tell her you want to see her."

"That should make her happy."

"I'll tell her you're coming by the club. She's more . . . relaxed at the club." Emily seemed to warm to the idea. "So you'll do it. You'll stop by?"

I said I would, and added, "I'll come when I get out."

18

They took the chest tube out the next afternoon, sewed me up, and then kept me a third day for observation. Norman came by on that third morning but I pretended to be asleep, and later in the day I saw Hock in the hallway, out of uniform, unshaven, wearing a silky Buffalo Bills jacket, jeans, and heavy work boots.

"Criminal," he said. "Patient-beater." He smiled knowingly. "It was Burnett, right? He tooled'm up?"

"Yeah."

"Well, Rolly calls every day. What's he expect?"

"I don't know."

"The guy's a fuckin drain on tax dollars. They oughtta give Jack a fuckin medal. What were you doin?"

"Nothin."

"Were you takin pictures?"

I looked away.

"You took pictures, didn't you?"

"Yeah."

"I knew it," he said. "Jesus. I knew it. I gotta get a copy of those." Then, lowering his voice, he took me by the arm above the elbow, guided me down the hall, and said, "Listen. I just saw something." He motioned more with his eyes than his head. "Over in surgical. They got a bottle of Dilaudid sittin on the counter."

"So what?"

"So it's a bottle of a hundred Dilaudid. Twenty dollars a pill."

"Where is it?"

"On the counter. Just sitting there. The nurse just got it from the pharmacy."

"You sure it's Dilaudid?"

"Yeah, I'm sure. I saw the guy delivering it. They're waitin for the nurse's aide or whatever the fuck she is to hand it off to. It's just sittin right there."

"And I guess you wanna take it."

"Mind reader."

"You need help? I'll help," I said.

He considered this for a moment.

"You sure, Frank?"

"Why not?"

He looked as if he didn't really want to involve me. Then he shrugged, glancing over his shoulder.

"I'll get the bottle. You just gotta do something."

"Something."

"Like distract her. Have a seizure."

"Oh come on."

"Well you know, try to kiss her."

"Oh my god."

"Well, see a car wreck out the window. I don't know. Anything."

"What'll you be doing?"

"I'm looking for a patient."

He hurried me on, guiding me.

"We got about three minutes, Frank. If you're in . . ."

"Why wouldn't I be?"

We walked toward the surgical unit. Hock stepped ahead. I stayed back a moment, then followed him through the double doors.

The SICU was set up like my own unit but opposite, with the beds stretching off to the left, the nurse's station at the front, and the windows along the far wall. As I walked in I saw Hock talking with a brusque, nasal-voiced woman. This was the charge nurse. I was supposed to distract her but she was already talking with Hock. She followed him down the aisle between the beds. Hock gestured as if he was going to see a patient, and she hurried after him, saying visiting hours were over, that he had to leave, etc. I walked along the curved counter of the nurse's station. It was filled with stacked charts, plastic racks, bins with blood tubes, syringes. Among all this I saw the bottle with the rectangular pharmacy sticker. The charge nurse followed Hock down the aisle. Hock kept walking. I figured I might as well grab the bottle myself. There was another nurse with her back turned, setting a drip rate. I wandered up to the counter and leaned over as if I was looking for something and I swept the bottle against my chest and stashed it beneath my shirt. An old man with jaundiced skin lay back watching me. I realized he was a patient I'd brought in. I just nodded to him and he nodded back to me and I turned and walked into the hallway. Rapid footsteps behind me. It was Hock.

"You got it?"

"Yeah."

"Give it," he hissed.

I handed him the bottle. He stashed it in his shirt without looking at it, then hurried into the stairway. I stopped at a drinking fountain.

"Hey. Hey you," someone said behind me.

It was the charge nurse. Fifty years old with long, thin, frayed, brownish hair, a lot of gray in it. I looked at her calmly.

"Who are you?" she demanded.

"Whattaya mean?"

"What's your name?"

"Frank."

"Were you . . ." She looked me up and down. "What were you doing back there? You were just in my unit."

"I wasn't doing anything. I'm bored. I was walking around."

I was wearing one of those open-backed hospital gowns. There was nowhere to hide a bottle. If it was in my shirt she'd have seen it.

"What's your full name?"

"Frank Verbeckas."

Her face changed. She recognized the name.

"Your brother's a surgeon?"

"Yes."

"You're EMS?"

"Yeah."

She looked at me uncertainly.

"I . . . I thought . . . something just happened."

She saw the exit to the stairs.

"Did you see someone go by?"

"I don't know. I was just walking around."

She frowned and ducked into the stairway. She came back and looked in the garbage. She entered the men's bathroom and came out a minute later and walked quickly to her unit. I left the doorway and went back to my bed and waited to see if anything else would happen. It didn't. After a while I started reading.

19

As I was changing into street clothes and cutting my hospital bracelet, two cops came into the ICU and walked down the aisle between beds. I recognized them, Cipatli and Dott, from the Thirty-Second Precinct. Dott was a short, easygoing black guy with a shaved head. The other guy, Cipatli, was a skinny Mexican with a pointy face, like a fish. Cipatli came up and said, "Bitch almost got you."

I asked if they'd found her.

"I ain't tryin to dampen your hopes or anything," Dott said. "But you know what the chances are of finding a crack-head when we don't even got her name? I wouldn't hold my breath, know what I mean?" He flipped a sheet on his little notebook and said, "One of the bystanders. A woman—"

"Yeah, I know."

"She filed a complaint. We got a statement from your partner."

"What'd he say?"

Cipatli, the Mexican guy, said, "Your partner said he was taking Rolly to the bus. Just bringing him in when some crackhead walks over, starts yelling, starts causing problems, and then she stabs you."

"That's right," I said. "That's exactly what happened."

Dott scribbled in his pad.

"He said you picked Rolly up in some alley."

"An abandoned building," I said. "One five two. Between Bradhurst and Douglas."

He scribbled.

"Your partner said you were just taking the guy out."

"We were just bringing him out to the bus."

"And she walks over?" Cipatli prompted me.

"Yeah, that's right."

"From where? From the stoop where she was sitting?"

"Right. From the stoop."

He went on writing.

"And she was with someone?" he guided me.

"Some church guy. Clean-cut. With a cross around his neck. A gold-chain thing."

"Yeah, we know the guy," Dott said.

"You didn't . . ." Cipatli hesitated. "Hit the church guy or nothin?"

"Nah. No way."

"Or your partner?"

"No."

"What about Rolly? They say he came in with a torn shirt. Was that from falling?"

"Yeah. He fell," I said. "He was drunk. And he fell. The guy's homeless. It's not a surprise he's wearing a torn shirt."

They nodded approvingly.

"After he tripped we were helping him up, and the crack-head came over. The other guy, the church guy, was talking to us while the crackhead got her knife."

"So the church guy distracted you?"

"You could say that."

"Even helped her in some way?"

"Yeah. He helped her."

"And you didn't touch the church guy?"

"No."

"And you didn't touch the patient?"

"Not except to help him."

"And then?"

"Then I was stabbed."

"So you were helping the patient. Rendering patient care. Doing your job. When the church guy interfered with you. Distracted you. And you were slashed from behind by the crackhead."

"Exactly," I said.

"Anything else?"

"No."

Dott scribbled one last thing, flipped the pad shut, and looked up.

"That oughtta do it."

"What'd Burnett say?" I asked again, and Dott said, "What you and your partner say corroborates completely. That oughtta do it," he said again, with emphasis, and I knew that nothing would happen with the complaint. I thanked them.

"Agh," Dott made a sound in his throat.

"Yeah, no problem," Cipatli said.

They seemed embarrassed even being there. When the police got shot we were the ones who treated them. As long as we didn't kill someone outright there wasn't much chance of a complaint going anywhere.

The two of them shook my hand and walked back up the aisles, both with their heads tilted, listening to their radios.

20

Down on one knee, I placed my head between the iron window bars. I saw an open area with cords and pulleys on the ceiling and long narrow strips about the length and width of a bowling alley. There were a few men in white in the far strip, darting back and forth with swords. Three young women with their masks off stood idly in the corner, talking. I walked over and tried the door. It was unlocked. I entered a passageway and there was a second door held open with a metal chair. Inside, Emily sat on a bench with one foot up, tying her white shoe. When she saw me she didn't even bother to shake my hand. She finished tying her shoe, put her foot down, stood, and turned into the club.

"You're early," she said. "Myra won't be here for an hour."

Emily started for the far end. I stood there. She came back.

"You don't wanna come?"

"Where?"

"You ever fence?"

I just looked at her.

"Well, it won't kill you. Come on."

Emily draped some leather smock over my head. It was heavy, like the lead apron at the dentist's. She gave me a foil, showed me how to hold it out, how to stand, and that was all the introduction I got. She edged forward in the crablike way that fencers move, clacked my foil on one side, clacked it on the other, and then surprised me by thrusting. I could feel the weight of the foil through the apron. She told me to hold the foil up again. I did. The same thing happened. Clack on one side, clack on the other, then she struck me in the chest, hard enough to knock me back.

"Jesus," I said.

"Can't hurt that much."

"Whatta you call that much?"

I showed her where my wound was. I told her not to hit outside the apron. She raised her foil.

"Yeah, don't worry about it," she said.

For the next hour she hit me all over, even on the shoulder and back a few times, but she did not come close to the wound. She had amazing dexterity with the foil. Once we started she did not talk to me at all. Her withdrawing manner dropped away with what seemed like relief, and she became impassioned, reckless. Bouncing back and forth, like an excited bird, she slashed with the foil. Slashed with it again. She let out little mad cries. Clack clack thrust. Clack clack thrust. Again and again she attacked with the light foil, striking impotently at the thick pad.

After an hour Myra came in. I waved to her but she just kept walking to the locker room. I felt myself flush. Emily, whose timid manner returned as soon as she lowered the foil, pretended not to notice. When Myra came out of the locker room she pulled her mask on and immediately started a bout. Emily walked over and Myra stopped, pulled off her mask, and they spoke with their backs to me. After a minute, in an impatient manner, Myra waved. I waved back. Then she started fencing again. Emily returned, smiling. "She's in the middle of a bout," she said. I figured there was no reason to go over and speak with her. I went on practicing with Emily, and Myra worked out for the entire afternoon at the other end of the club.

21

It was Sunday and Norman and I had gone out to Queens to see Dad. He was lying there with white marble over him, leaves on the grass all around, and piled up in drifts near the headstone. We each had rakes, working with our backs to each other.

"A nurse from surgical talked to me," Norman said.

I was quiet, drawing the rake through the grass.

"Yeah," I said. "So what?"

"She was talking about a bottle of Dilaudid." He placed the rake in the grass as if he'd go back to work. Then he lifted it again. "Are you a junkie?"

"I don't take that shit," I said. He was quiet, raking. "I did it for money."

He paused, gripping and regripping the rake. I felt him looking at me.

"You got caught, I couldn't've helped you," he said.

"I didn't ask you to," I said.

He pulled the rake through grass. I didn't say anything more about it and neither did he, but by the jerky way he moved I could tell he was thinking about it. After a while he said, "What happened to the pictures?"

"Whatta you mean, what happened to them? Nothing happened to them. I developed them. That's it."

I could tell what he was thinking.

"I was just helping a friend out with the Dilaudid. It's not because of the pictures."

"I didn't say it was."

"The pictures are crap, but I got a few of him that are o.k. I'm glad to have them. He looks happy."

"I'm sure you want to think that."

"I just said that's the way he looked. Not that he was happy. And not that it makes any difference," I added. "It's obvious he wasn't. Do you think it's not obvious?"

The metal tines of Norman's rake scracked against the hard ground. I pulled dark leaves into a sodden clump. The weight of cold leaves against my hip as I hauled a sack to the trash. Bare branches spread against the sky. The clouds were high and in long thin ridges. I sat some distance away on the frozen ground, looking up through branches in the dwindling light. Norman was working his way around a tree with a hoe, hacking at the hard earth, loosening it up to plant bulbs. I closed my eyes and listened to the hoe cutting into the soil. He was working furiously, with more effort than it really required. I was cold. I got up. The headstone was stained with bird droppings. In the dim light it looked very dark, and the droppings very bright, very white. I brought my camera out and took a photograph. Norman turned, holding the hoe.

"Nice, Frank," he said. "He'd like that."

"I don't think he'd mind," I said.

22

She was waiting at the edge of the dry fountain, that navy sweatshirt in a lump beside her.

"You got your camera?" she asked.

"Yeah."

"I saw something. You can take a picture of it."

We walked toward West Third.

"What is it?"

"You'll see. You'll like it."

We got to the corner of the park and she pointed at the

street. It was a pigeon squashed by a car. A red smear on concrete, with a few feathers.

"Aw Jesus," I said.

"What?"

"Some dead animal. I don't want a picture of that."

"I guess if that was a person you'd be more interested."

"It would be a more interesting subject, anyway."

She made a little sound in her throat and crooked her head. She seemed disappointed. After a moment, in a different tone, she said, "Come on. I need an ice."

We walked down West Third Street. We looked at CDs and tapes spread out on the sidewalk, and then went on to Saint Mark's where we stopped at one of the outdoor arcades and played Ms. Pac-Man. I sucked at videogames, didn't care about them, and was killed three times in less than two minutes. She was better, and as she played I watched her grow fierce, competitive, like when she fenced, though, at the end, when the blue demons began to move very fast, and the sound grew loud and ominous, and it seemed hopeless, she suddenly held her hands from the controls, closed her eyes, and only knew she'd been eaten from the sound. She turned to me, smiling sheepishly. "I can't stand to see it," she said. A minute later we went over to an Italian bakery on Second Avenue where they sold ices, but we'd dawdled too long with the CDs and the videogame and they were locking the door just as we arrived. Emily banged on the window. She dropped her bag and banged on it again. A waiter inside went by without looking.

"He hears me. He pretends he doesn't hear."

She kicked the door, the waiter looked up, and we ran

partway down the block. The waiter, a fifty-year-old Italian guy with slicked hair and a rounded belly covered by an apron, stepped out. "Hey, kick this!" he bellowed, stood defiantly a moment, then saw Emily coming back and turned. He locked himself inside the store and smiled through the glass. Emily kicked the door, then saw me watching her and was suddenly sheepish again, shy. She hurried back, saying, "I really wanted an ice." We crossed Houston and went on toward the Lower East Side. She lived in a four-story building with a fire escape up front, graffiti on the door, and garbage cans lined up in the entrance. We walked into a long, thin apartment with a small kitchen to the left and her bedroom at the end of a dim hallway, where a bicycle leaned against the wall. There were dirty clothes everywhere. Old soda cans, old soda cups with straws, six or seven coffee cups with dried grounds at the bottom, fast food bags crumpled and left on the floor, books and newspapers everywhere. She lay back on a futon and said, "You ever been to Norway?"

"No."

"I've been thinking of going to Norway. They got these fjords there. Like these little passageways of water. Really pretty. Really scenic. Like you can't believe how nice they are. You read that book *Mysteries*?"

"Nah."

"It's set in Norway. I'm thinking of going there."

She showed me the book, *Mysteries,* that she'd spoken of, and while I was looking at it she said, "How old are you?"

"Twenty-three."

"I'm twenty-one. I've never been anywhere. I figure, better go now, you know. While I'm healthy." She massaged her leg. "Cramps," she said. "I gotta drink more water." Then, "My father lives in Norway. I haven't seen him for like . . . thirteen years or something. But I thought, you know, why not? It's gotta be nice. Snow. Clean little towns. Norway."

There were a few large pillows along the wall near the radiator. I sat.

"Your mom there?"

"Dead. Kidneys," she said.

"My dad's dead, too," I said.

Her face darkened. I figured Myra must have said something. Emily picked a speck from the sheet and tossed it toward the window.

"Myra told you," I guessed.

"She said you had a picture."

I felt around in my jacket pocket and dropped the print near her leg. She held it up. Studied it for a while.

"He looks like a good guy."

"Yeah, he was a nice guy. He wouldn't've wanted to hurt anyone."

She set the print on the sheet. She nodded, as if deciding something.

"That's how you got into medicine," she said.

"I don't know."

"Your brother's a doc, right?"

"Yeah."

"You had these family troubles. And so you wanted to help other people."

"You should see how I help," I said.

"I think that's it," she said. Then, "Your mom still around?"

"She's still alive." I made a motion like I was smoking a joint. "They weren't together long. She lives in Washington State. I don't talk to her much."

"At least you got a brother."

"At least," I said.

She opened a *New Yorker,* the cover marked with a mosaic of moon-shaped arcs—perfectly rounded stains from the bottom of a coffee mug. There was a battered boombox on the mantel of an old fireplace. Tapes without cases scattered around it. Mostly stuff that was popular on college radio stations at the time—Cure, R.E.M., Lou Reed, Replacements—music that I knew, too. I put on *Nothing's Shocking* and she went on with her *New Yorker.* I found a photography book against the wall beneath the window. It looked like it had been rained on, and still had a library card in it, due about eight months before. We read for a while, not talking much. When the tape was over she got up and flipped it and went back to reading. Then held the magazine across her chest and lay back.

"You're looking at the Winogrand?"

"Yeah."

"You like it?"

"He's great. It's depressing he's so good. I'll never be that good."

"I get like that with the fencing. Overwhelmed. Intimidated."

She rolled the magazine and tapped it in her hand.

"You know a lot about it? The photographs?"

"Just what I like."

"Who do you like?"

"Arbus, Evans, Weegee, Golden, Hujar . . ."

She nodded. She'd never heard of any of them. She didn't pretend she had.

"Well, I'd go see em at the Met. Take a look. You want to?"

I said I did.

I stayed at her apartment for an hour. When I decided to go she just waved from the bed, didn't even try to get up to shake my hand.

"It was good seeing you, Frank."

"Good seeing you, Emily."

"Shut the door behind you," she said when I was in the hallway.

I pulled the door shut. When I was a few floors down I heard the bolt turning.

23

Leaning against the wall of the loading bay, Hock went through the photographs of Burnett and Rolly, holding a few up into the dim light, hiding the prints from the other medics when they walked past. Not that they would have cared. With the crack wars and the crime explosion, we saw it all. A few pictures were nothing. Hock looked at the shot of Burnett with his forearm around Rolly's neck.

"Looks like he's strangling him," Hock said, laughing. He

straightened the prints and said, "Burnett says you're seeing that HIV girl?"

"That what he said?"

"He says he saw her with you in the hospital. He says you're fucking her."

"I'm seeing her friend," I said. "Not her."

"Well, Burnett says it wasn't her friend visiting you."

"She was at the clinic that day. She just came to visit."

"Ah," Hock said.

I wasn't sure if he believed me or not.

"She saw me on the news," I added.

"Came up to see the patient-beater?"

"Something like that."

Hock lit a cigarette. He smoked with the cigarette between his first two fingers so when he inhaled it was like he was putting a hand over his mouth.

"You heard they made a new regulation," he said. "After that Dilaudid thing. Nurses can't pass on the medication. Has to go straight to the patient."

"Nah, I didn't know that."

"You did a good job."

"It was nothing."

"It was quick thinking. You were pretty cool about it."

I shrugged, but inside I warmed from the praise.

"That nurse talked to you?" he asked.

I said she did.

"You mention me?"

"Fuck no."

"Did she know I was EMS?"

"I doubt it."

He looked at me for a moment.

"We'll have something else going on soon. Some real thing."

I was quiet.

"Not that I'd blame you for tellin me to fuck off. But damn . . . You're a natural."

I couldn't help smiling.

"Talk to me later."

"Yeah yeah. All right. We'll talk about it later."

He seemed relieved in a way. I think there was a part of him that felt guilty about getting me involved. But there was another part that thought, Why not? He ground his cigarette on the concrete.

"You sure you ain't with the AIDS girl?"

"Yeah, I'm sure."

"You ain't kissed her or nothin?"

"No."

He hesitated.

"She a junkie?"

"I don't think so."

"White girl, college girl, how'd she get it?"

"I don't even know."

"Well, if she's a junkie I know someone who can hook her up. You might even make yourself a commission."

24

A four-story brownstone and Burnett and I walked up the stairway slowly. We could smell our patient from the lobby, and with each floor the smell grew stronger, more stifling. At the third floor a cop in uniform leaned out a window, waving fresh air toward his face. Above him, from an open door, his partner bolted out with a hand over his mouth, and clambered past us, panting, "The dog got to him."

Deadpan, Burnett turned, and said, "Think we can save him, Frank?"

A few black flies buzzed into the hallway. Burnett set the equipment on the stairs.

"You wanna go?" he asked, and before I could answer, he said, "Why the fuck'm I asking? Of course you wanna go."

As I stepped past the cop, he said, "You're about three days too late."

I entered a hallway thirty feet long, with an open doorway at the end. The floor was dotted with piles of feces. Everywhere there were large brown print marks. A mad scraping of claws on tiles. Behind a locked door, a repetitive thudding at waist height. A deep, short, angry bark. I checked the door to make sure it was locked, then tiptoed onward. As I neared the far room I got an obstructed view of dark bare legs. I could hear the dog behind me, whining, scrabbling. I reached for my camera. Through the viewfinder the entire shape of the man came into view. I stepped up to him—focused, objective, alert—and began taking pictures.

25

Walking along the East River near the Williamsburg Bridge.

"So how'd you get it?"

She answered without hesitating.

"The normal way. I slept with someone."

"Someone you knew well?"

"Not really," she said.

The concrete out there was tilted and uneven. Weeds grew up in cracks, and the London planes, which lost their leaves early, were stark, bare. The abandoned factories were dark and silent on the other side of the river.

"He was a fencing coach."

"Ah."

"One of the seasonal guys. I wasn't a prude or anything. I liked him, he liked me. We were drunk. It happened."

"You'd think he'd tell you," I said.

"We were drunk," she said again, as if that excused him. "The chances aren't that great. He probably thought it wouldn't happen."

She tossed a pebble at the metal rail that ran along the river. The pebble tinged and skipped into the water.

"How long before you found out?"

"I was a senior. He was already dead. So it was hard to be angry at him. You know, him being dead."

"Had you been with anyone else?"

"Not so they'd get it."

She tossed a pebble at the smooth trunk of a maple. She missed the trunk. She found another pebble and tossed it. She missed again. I tossed a pebble and hit the trunk.

"Ya bastard," she said.

She tried a third time with a pebble. Again she missed. I hit it. I'd won the tossed pebble game. She swore and swatted my arm, then squeezed it. We started walking. I could feel the place she'd squeezed. We walked side by side.

"What'd you do afterwards?" I asked.

"I didn't do anything." She picked pebbles here and there from the sidewalk. "I didn't do what he did, though. I always told people. I never hid it."

"Did they want to be with you after that? After you told them?"

"No," she said. "Not really."

She stopped and nodded toward a tree trunk.

"You ready?"

I said I was, and we both tossed pebbles.

We walked up and down the riverbank, along the green, oily water, talking about her illness, and then moving past the subject. When she bent down to pick up pebbles I noticed how small and deft her hands were. Dark stones piled up in her little white palm.

26

She sat at the kitchen table in a neatly kept apartment in Washington Heights. A shelf of colored glass knickknacks in the opening between the kitchen and living room, a photograph of the woman, as a girl, in front of canefields and surrounded by a large family, only a few of them wearing shoes. I noticed a black leather briefcase in the hallway, a fancy umbrella with a wooden handle, a framed MBA diploma from NYU on the wall. The woman herself looked exhausted, ashen; I went into the bathroom to see the bowl filled with black liquid, and as I came back out Burnett was holding a bottle of Extra Strength Tylenol. He shook it to show it was empty.

"The whole bottle," he said. "Three days ago." Then, "What's it look like?"

"Tar. Ink," I said, and he nodded.

"Another success story," he said.

The woman did not look up when we came back into the doorway. She had a little overnight bag at her feet, and a manila folder with computer printouts of her entire medical history so we did not have to ask her any questions.

"Looks like you've been through this before," Burnett said. "Let's go."

She was quiet in the back of the ambulance, and I was quiet sitting on the bench. I read her entire medical history and copied the information I needed onto my paperwork. I thought she did not want me to talk, and I didn't really want to talk to her, but as we neared the hospital she looked up and said, "So that's it? I'm dying?"

I could see she wanted to know.

"I think you are," I said.

"I've tried before."

"I saw that," I said. "You used aspirin before. A bottle of aspirin won't kill you. But twenty of those Tylenol could do it. And you took fifty."

She nodded slowly.

"They won't be able to save me?"

"If you'd come in when you first took them they could have. Now you have no liver function. They'll try to get you a transplant."

"Can I refuse?"

"Yes. They won't want to waste a liver if you don't want it."

She did not say anything to this, but faintly, she smiled, and turned her head. Again, she was quiet. So was I. We were passing the George Washington Bridge.

"Are you glad?" I asked, after a moment. "Now that you've done it, that it's inevitable, do you regret it?"

"Why would I?"

This answer pleased me.

27

Washington Square Park at dusk. I had high-speed film if I needed it, but I didn't see anyone I really wanted to take a shot of. I just kept circling around, scanning the park, looking over at Coles Gymnasium, where I knew Emily worked out sometimes. I thought I wanted to call her and I also thought I shouldn't call her. Once I stopped at the pay phone near the library and lifted the receiver, but then I remembered us walking along the river and the way she'd touched my arm. I hung up without dialing and went back to my apartment and into the darkroom. I turned on the safelight. I could have worked on some prints but I didn't feel like it. I drank a beer slowly. I thought I might cry, felt it welling up inside me, but then it didn't come. I lay there without doing anything, one arm thrown over my head, lips parted, staring at the ceiling.

28

All the trees were bare. Everyone wore winter jackets, hats, and scarves. Burnett and I were at 157th and Broadway, watching the women come from the subway.

"You haven't seen her?" Burnett said.

"Fuck no."

"Haven't even talked to her?"

"Not for . . . almost two weeks."

"What happened?"

"Nothing happened."

"You fuck her and get scared?"

"Nah."

"You kiss her?"

"Nah, nah. Never touched her."

"I'm surprised, Frank. Way you are. Thought you'd be into it."

"What do you mean, *into* it?"

"I mean you like sick people. That turns you on."

I didn't say anything.

"Admit it, Frank"

"I don't know if I need to admit it or not."

"Well, it's true." He put a hand behind his neck. His big, square, yellowed teeth showed over his brown goatee. "So what'd you say to her?"

"I didn't say anything."

"You must've said something."

"I just stopped calling her."

"That's the best way. Don't explain. Just stop talking. End of story." He watched some young woman with a brief-case in a business suit walk out of the subway. "I don't have anything against her. But . . . if she's positive, she needs to find someone else who's positive. And you ask me, she seemed dumb anyway."

"Why do you say that?"

"Cause she didn't wanna go to court. She coulda made a lotta fuckin money, but she just said fuck it. You ask me, that's pretty dumb," he said.

29

"You can take me home."

"All right," I said.

"I'm not . . . trying to take advantage or anything. You asked if I needed anything."

"I know what I said. I meant it. Here." I felt his hand on my arm. He was blind. We walked slowly from the park. "You don't have a dog?"

"I can't afford the food."

"Medicare won't cover it?"

"You making some kind of joke?" he said. "Anyway, I got a cane. Cane's as good as a dog if you know where you're going. I don't need no seeing-eye dog."

He lived three or four blocks away. Some apartment on Carmine Street. He'd probably been there fifty years. In the lobby he let go of my arm and went to the mailboxes, found his box by touch, inserted the key, got his mail, and then shut it. He started up the stairway holding on to the railing, not saying anything.

"Are you coming?" he said when he was halfway up.

"Yes," I said, and hurried after him.

I followed him into his apartment. In the living area there was a large table with many stacked papers, books in Braille, and a radio. As soon as he entered he reached for the coatrack, found it, and hung up his jacket. I tried to help him but he went on himself.

"I know where it is. I know my own apartment. As long as nothing's moved."

He walked to the windows, which were heavily draped, and beneath them ran a long, low table lined with wigs on Styrofoam heads. Blond, brunette, redhead, curly, straight, permed. Nine different wigs. He felt his way along from the wall and took the third from the left, a red-haired wig. He set it on the coffee table in front of the couch and ran his fingers through the wig slowly, his head up, tilted at an angle.

"It's hair," he said.

"I know what it is."

"I mean, it's real hair. Feel it."

I put my fingers in the fine red hair. A certain ache opened up inside me.

"They were my wife's," he said.

"Was she blind?"

"No. She was always knocking things about. Even more than me. Moving everything around. But not blind."

"She's—"

"Eighty-eight," he said. "Two years ago. I got rid of all her things. It was too cluttered. But I kept her hair." He bent down and sniffed. "You can still smell her. Hair holds a smell."

"Can I take a picture of that?"

"Yeah, sure. That's what you're here for, right?"

"Yes."

"What do you want me to do?"

"Just like that. Just stay like that."

I took the shot quickly before he moved.

"Can you feel the flash?" I asked him afterward.

"No. I'm completely blind. I can hear the shutter. But I see nothing. And the flash doesn't have weight. Not like sound."

I took pictures for ten minutes. I got him feeling the hair, sniffing it, sitting calmly along the row of wigs. When I was done I sat back with the camera on the table.

"You're leaving now?" he asked me.

"If you want me to."

"Stay," he said.

"I'll stay a minute."

He made coffee, measuring the grounds, pouring hot water into a French press. He knew where everything was. And I watched it all openly, studying him. I wondered if he could feel me watching, if that had weight.

"How old are you?" he asked.

"Twenty-three."

"Agh," he waved a hand at me. "You should be out. Meeting people. Having a good time." He held his hands up. "Come here," he said. I got up and took a step. "No. Right here." He reached up and felt my face. He bent my head down and smelled my hair, then let me go. "What do you do? Do you have a job?"

"Paramedic."

"An exciting life."

"I guess."

"Well, this is my life. What you see here. This is it."

"It seems like a good one."

"I know bullshit when I hear it."

"Really," I said. "I see a lot of people. You're not doing too bad."

I put my camera away. I said I was going.

"Send me a copy."

I shook his hand. A dry, strong grip. He held me a moment. When he let go I stepped outside his doorway. I heard him locking the door behind me.

Half a floor down a potted geranium rested on the windowsill, and through the dirty window, a garbage-littered courtyard. Someone was calling Frankie, Frankie, Frankie, from a window further up. I waited until the calling stopped. Then I walked down slowly.

30

Hock and I entered the little lobby of Kagans Liquors.

"How much money you got?" Hock asked me. "We could get that Rumpleminze shit."

"Yeah o.k."

"Or you want Seagrams? That sound better?"

"Whatever."

"Don't know why I'm asking. You don't give a fuck."

"I'd go with the pint," some aged, diminutive man said behind us.

"That right?"

"Other's too sweet. Fuck your stomach up."

"Take it from the expert," Hock said to me, and the older guy nodded, seeing it as a compliment. This guy was not much more than five feet tall, with an underbite and crooked yellowed teeth that stuck up a quarter-inch above his lower lip. He wore thick glasses with black rims and his right thumb jutted out at an angle as if it had been broken and healed incorrectly. Hock eyed him, then pulled his medic cap down, showing him.

"I brought you in, haven't I?" Hock said.

"Probably."

"I brought you in drunk."

"Probably," the old man said.

"How you doin? You gonna be sick tonight?"

"I guess we'll have to see bout that. For both of us," he added.

"Guess that's right," Hock said.

The clerk came back with the Seagrams in a bag. Thick, graffiti-covered glass surrounded the register. We handed the money through the revolving door and the Seagrams was given back with change.

Outside the store Hock threw the bag on the ground. It was late, about midnight, and there were only a few people wandering back and forth on the sidewalk. Some guy sprawled below the neon sign with an empty two-dollar bottle.

"You wanna go first?" Hock said.

I didn't know what he was talking about. I was fingering a paper cup. I held it out, like he'd pour me some, but he just gripped the pint and put his thumb halfway. "This's yours," he said, indicating the lower half. Then, keeping his thumb on that spot, he tilted the bottle up and drank for about fifteen seconds. When he lowered it his eyes were watery and the liquid sloshed at the exact level of his thumb. He wiped his mouth with the back of his hand and screwed the cap back on, handing me the bottle.

"Rest is yours," he said.

"Jesus," I said.

The older guy with the underbite came out of the store. He looked at me holding the half-empty bottle. A yellow-toothed grin as he raised his own.

"You be careful out there, ya hear?"

"Yeah yeah," Hock said.

We walked toward the loading bays where there was a group of medics waiting—Burnett, a Dominican guy named Rogero, a Haitian named Geroux. Others came and went. There was a bottle of rum, upright, on the hood of Hock's Buick. Stacked paper cups upside down. We'd been gone about five minutes. Geroux looked at the half-empty pint.

"That wasn't me," I said.

Hock stood calmly, an eyebrow cocked. Geroux, who was a short guy with a little black mustache, put a hand on Hock's shoulder.

"You better take't easy, my man."

"Fuck it. I'll sleep'n the car."

"There you go," Burnett said, and, taking the pint from me, tilted it quickly. He handed the pint back and I drank, then turned away. I made a face.

"Look't Frank."

"Yeah, I know."

"You better stick ta Budweiser, my man."

Hock poured rum into a paper cup and took a small sip. He looked away, spit.

"Go on. Drink," Rogero said to Hock. "You ain't got no one waitin."

Geroux seemed mildly surprised.

"Thought you were married."

"Was," Hock said. "No more."

Rogero tapped his cup.

"Welcome to the club."

"That's right," Burnett said in a boisterous way.

Hock gave Burnett a withering glance.

"I don't know what you're yappin about."

"You're married," Rogero said resentfully. "You got a kid."

"On the way," Burnett said. "That's why I gotta . . ."

He drank.

Hock stood back with his thumbs in his belt, swaying a little. I was leaning against the car. I was usually pretty quiet in a group. Geroux shook his cup out, crushed it, and tossed it at my feet.

"You ain't married, are you, Frank?"

"Nah."

"You got a girlfriend?"

"Nah."

Burnett smiled broadly.

"He's fuckin some HIV girl."

"Aw shit," Rogero said.

Hock was smiling, too.

"Are you?"

"Nah," I said. "I was just talking to her."

They all laughed. Geroux leaned over, holding the tip of the bottle out.

"You doin that you better drink up, my man."

He poured in my cup.

"I'm not doing anything," I said, and they all laughed again.

It made me feel good to have them think I was doing something with her.

Burnett reached over and grabbed the neck of the bottle.

"Gimme that," he said. "Once the kid comes—"

Across the street, at the station, ambulances were lined up in the lot. From time to time medics jumped in their ambulances and sped away, the sirens sounding, and a hand held out the window, waving as they passed. Sometimes, after a job, they came over and joined us. We all drank for about twenty minutes and then Rogero said, "You all ready?"

"I guess we better be," Burnett said.

"Shit," Hock said, motioning with his cup. "It'll only be seconds and thirds."

"You think I give a fuck?" Burnett said.

He took the bottle of rum and poured into each of our cups, then hurled the empty bottle at the green Dumpster. It shattered against the side.

"Ah shit," Geroux said. "I see where this's goin."

We all walked down the block with our paper cups and then cut west on 138th Street. A metal staircase led into a concrete channel between two buildings. The staircase rocked as we clambered down. Burnett dropped his cup. At the bottom he retrieved it, drank the last few drops, and tossed it aside.

To our right there was a doorway propped open with merengue music coming out. A guy I knew, Henry Penna-chio, stood in the door, counting money.

"Fifteen bucks," he said.

"Aw fuck," Burnett said.

"You knew it," Hock said. "So shut the fuck up."

"Pay the man," Geroux said.

"I better get my money's worth," Burnett said.

"Yeah, don't worry about it," Pennachio said.

We heard voices, shouting.

"They already here?"

"Fuck yeah they're here. They been being here an hour."

"Pay the man," Geroux shouted.

Burnett said he only had ten bucks. Everyone started yelling behind him. Pennachio hesitated, then said fuck't, and took the money. The rest of us had the fifteen. We walked through a dark hallway that turned right, then opened into a large area with exposed pipes and three or four bare bulbs lighting it. There was no furniture or anything. Just a concrete floor, a long drain down the middle, and an old washing machine pushed up against the wall. A boombox sat on the floor with some tapes resting on top. There were about thirty men inside, medics from the station, cops we knew from the Thirtieth and Thirty-Second Precincts, some of Hock's friends. Wandering among the crowd of men were six prostitutes from the neighborhood, dressed in short skirts that cut off at the thigh. One of them stood along the wall wearing a bikini bottom and a jean jacket, not buttoned, and nothing on underneath. Rogero walked up to her and reached inside her jacket and they moved toward the corner where there were sheets hung from the ceiling, making a little closed-off area. Beyond the sheets shadows moved.

"Ah fuck," Hock said. "They weren't kiddin."

I walked past everyone slowly, some people I knew nodding at me.

"Frank," they said, and I went on.

Against the far wall I saw a tall Hispanic woman with swollen breasts. She was lactating. Burnett was talking to her, squeezing her breasts, making the milk come out.

"Look at this, Frank," he said. "Like a fuckin cow."

She smacked his hands.

I walked out the back door into a little alleyway. A fence lined with shrubs made a sheltered area where a blanket was spread in the dirt. Obviously someone had been sleeping there. I looked at that blanket and then I sat on it. After a while I lay flat in that hidden spot. I could hear music from the basement faintly. The door swung open and a silhouette appeared. It was Hock. He walked over. Kicked my leg with his boot.

"You sick?"

"Nah, I'm not sick."

"What the fuck you doin then?"

"Nothin."

"You paid your fifteen bucks. You don't wanna go inside?"

"I will in a minute."

Hock sipped from his paper cup. He spit over the fence.

"Well, you look pretty fuckin weird. Layin there in the dirt."

"I'm o.k.," I said, and Hock made a face like he didn't believe it.

He went back to the party, and I listened to the muted music, distant voices, and beyond that, to the north, the sound of a siren turning deep and sad before it faded.

31

Dogs of all shapes and sizes leapt and snarled and tumbled in the dog park, while the owners, along the edge, sat on benches, watching. Emily stood at the fence and pretended she did not see me coming. She only looked up at the last moment, motioning inside the fence with the white end of a broken twig.

"They do everything for their dogs. Bring them places. Buy them things."

"It's embarrassing."

"It's not embarrassing. It's what they want to give each other."

She brushed her hands on the back of her pants, then made a vague gesture with her right hand—the beginnings of a parry in fencing.

"Have you taken their pictures?"

"The dogs? No."

"The owners?"

I shook my head.

"It's not like that with me."

"Like what?"

"I just take pictures of what I'm interested in. I don't make statements."

A tennis ball shivered the fence links. A writhing knot of fur and dust overtook the wet ball. Dust floating away slowly. She looked at the place where the ball had been.

"I have some new pictures. I'll show you," I said.

I took out a shot of a Styrofoam face, old hands on straight hair, and the distant, blank eyes of the blind man.

"That's better than the dogs," she said.

Something resentful in the way she said it. She had not looked me in the eye the whole time, and I could tell she was angry. I hadn't talked to her for three weeks. She placed a foot on the green metal armrest of a bench. She untied then began to tie her shoe. With her hands holding the two laces, not moving, she said, "I called you."

"I know you did."

"I thought maybe you were angry."

"About what?"

"The lawyer," she said simply, glancing up, then looking back at her shoe. "I thought maybe you were waiting to see if I'd go with him. When you saw I wouldn't—"

"I don't care about that."

"Are you sure?"

"Yeah, I'm sure."

Eyes lowered, she went on tying her shoe, then stepped ahead of me.

"I thought maybe you did," she said.

I walked with my head turned away.

"Now you're smiling," she said.

"I just think it's funny you thought I was thinking about the lawyer. I'm the exact person who doesn't care about that."

She saw I was telling the truth. We turned from the dog park and walked on the concrete path lined with green benches. Beneath maples and London planes there were older men with canes, couples sitting close, chess players with their hinged boxes. She did not say anything else for a minute, but something in her loosened. She seemed happy. A pretty teenaged girl with a textbook open turned a page as we passed.

"When I was a student I'd come out here to study. I couldn't sit ten minutes without someone coming up. Even in that last year they'd do it. College girl alone in the park. I'd get annoyed and think of going with them. As a punishment."

"Did you?"

"No, no. Not the kind of thing you do."

An athletic-looking man in his thirties stood in front of the schoolgirl. Swaggered a little. The girl looked up from her book, curling a strand of blond hair behind her ear. Beyond them, the swirling activity of the dog park was muted by distance.

"We could get a drink," Emily said suddenly.

"I'd get a drink," I said.

Walking toward the East Village, we paused at several bars, and finally we stopped in front of Holiday. She rolled an empty bottle away with her foot.

"Frank," she said, and I could tell she didn't want to get a drink anymore. She said, "I'm sick, Frank. I ought not to. For a second I thought, Who cares? Why not? But I shouldn't be drinking. Can we go to the park?"

"I like the park," I said.

"Not much fun for you."

"If you saw the fun I normally have, you wouldn't feel bad."

We walked past the bars, talking idly, and it all came back at once. We were friends. It seemed silly not to have called her. As we approached Houston she said, "I thought maybe you found a girlfriend or something. Did you?"

"Are you kidding?"

She crossed the street with her head down and we spent an hour along the river. It began to drizzle and soon it was raining in earnest. A gray, steady rain. We left the park and walked single-file along buildings. I figured we were going back to her place, but I wasn't sure. I was cold. I could see my breath. Emily wore a green knit hat with a white stripe. We stopped in the arched doorway of a four-story brownstone. She took her hat off and squeezed. Brown water came out. She pulled the wet hat over her wet head and a man looked at us through the first-floor window. A minute later he came out and told us we couldn't stand there, that we had to move on, that it was private property. We went down the block beneath construction scaffolding. She took her hat off again. Her hair clung to her forehead. Beneath the scaffolding there was a middle-aged woman with a paper bag stained dark at the top. She was doing the same thing as us, trying to wait out the rain. She set her bag down roughly and tried to light a cigarette with a wet lighter—snick snick snick snick—damn—snicksnick—and finally it lit. She wiped her palm on the inside of her jacket and stepped out. Emily and I went west with dirty brown water running along curbs into grates. It grew dim and the air turned a grayish-blue color. The streetlights came on. It began to rain harder. All the buildings in that area were being converted into residential lofts. We stopped at the gutted shell of a warehouse and walked up the stoop to the first floor, where old bricks were half-covered with new plasterboard. There were buckets of spackling compound placed here and there haphazardly. There was no front door. Emily and I stood in the hallway.

"What made you call finally?" she asked.

"I just wanted to."

She looked like she thought it was something else.

"Not like there's so many things I want," I said, and she considered this for a moment, then said, "At least you didn't give me some bullshit story."

She was shivering. I offered her my jacket but she shrugged my hands off. She drew a line in plaster dust with her boot. She took a couple of steps toward the door and slicked hair off her forehead and picked up a rusting iron rod that was used to support the concrete. She whisked it about, then studied the pattern her feet left in the dust. She did not look at me. She stood in the door so slanting rain drops fell on her. She stepped back a few feet. I eased past her and she turned as I did.

"You have your camera with you?" she asked.

"I always do."

"It's a nasty day for taking pictures."

We were standing on either side of the doorway. I found the metal rod. It was heavier than I thought. Rough on the fingers. I waved it in the air, then balanced it against the wall gently and wiped my hand on my pants leg. We were standing in the half-light with the rain pattering outside and then we were kissing and had been kissing for ten minutes. My mind went away and I remember coming back, slowly, like after anesthesia.

"This is all we can do. You know that," she said.

"I know."

"You know this, even this, can be dangerous. You can't bite me."

"I'm not going to bite you. Be quiet."

We leaned against the wall. We kissed in the blue dusky light. The room darkened. A while later she said, "You can walk back with me, but you can't come up."

"I don't want to come up," I said. "I'll walk you back."

We walked with our arms around each other. We stopped where the man in the window had spoken to us and when I looked up he was watching. I felt tremendously happy. I did not want to let go of her, not even for a moment. We stepped into puddles instead of separating. I didn't know we were close to her building until we were right there. Dark, wet brick looming over us. We stopped in the doorway.

"We'll stand here a minute. I won't come up," I said.

Ten minutes later she unlocked the front door, and we went up.

32

I woke and realized she was awake, too. It was still dark out. Maybe three or four hours had passed. Raindrops spattered intermittently on the windowpane. Water had pooled on the windowsill and there was reflected light on the ceiling. Outside, long low clouds, colored orange, slid by quickly. It was clearing.

"Did you hear the thunder?" she asked.

"I was asleep."

"There was thunder. I wanted to open the window." She leaned over me. "Do you mind if I open the window?"

The heat had not been turned on in the building. It couldn't have been more than forty degrees in the bedroom. We lay close beneath the sheet and the blanket, not touching. In the dark we heard the sound of trucks crossing the seams of the Williamsburg Bridge. Intermittent clacks and thumps. I felt her shift beneath the covers.

"You regret it now," she said.

"I don't regret it," I said. "Just the opposite. I feel really good."

She saw I meant it, and seemed surprised. A sort of warmth spread through her slowly. I felt her hand on my side beneath the sheet. She lay closer to me. After a while I went to the bathroom and when I came back she was lying naked on the bed with her arms thrown over her head. She was a little stiff, trying not to be self-conscious.

"You have your camera, Frank? I don't mind. Take my picture."

I stood looking down at her.

"No," I said.

33

It was a few days later, and the rain had turned to snow. Hock leaned back against the wall of the loading bay, smoking a cigarette. Burnett had his arms crossed.

"You're a dumbfuck, Frank. You said it wasn't happening."

"I know what I said."

"You said it wasn't, and it did."

"Well."

"He says well. Good answer, Frank."

"I don't know what else to say other than I did it, and I feel pretty good about it."

"I believe that," Burnett said. He looked at Hock. "You listenin to this?"

"Yep," Hock said.

"He's a dumb fuck, right?"

"Depends on how you look at it. Frank likes sick people. He gets off on it. In that way he showed some sense."

"It's not like that," I said quietly.

"Gimme a fuckin break," Burnett said. "You even use a condom?"

"Oh, shut up."

"It's a legitimate question," Hock said.

"Yeah, I used a condom."

Hock made a conciliatory gesture.

"So he used a condom," Burnett said. "So the fuck what? It's still fuckin stupid. A million healthy girls. Frank's gotta pick one that's infected." Burnett touched my bag with the toe of his boot. "You got that picture of the kid, Frank?"

"Which one?"

He pointed to his forehead. I knew which one he meant. I searched around and found it. I gave it to him. He turned it for me to see.

"Take a look, Frank. That's what you got to look forward to. Coming attractions."

"Nice, Jack."

I took the print from him and without looking at it put it back in its place. Hock was smoking silently. Beyond the loading bay it was snowing. Practically a whiteout. Really coming down. Hock hit my shoulder with the back of his hand.

"Come on," he said.

"What?"

"I wanna talk to you."

"You're talking to him now," Burnett said.

"I wanna talk to him alone."

"Knock some sense into him," Burnett said, but he looked unhappy. It hurt Burnett's feelings when he was not included in the conversation. He pulled his hood on and stomped out into the snow. Hock frowned at the place where Burnett had been.

"I don't give a fuck what you do, Frank. And I know you don't care what other people think. I appreciate the apathy. But don't pretend this isn't stupid."

"I admitted it in the first place."

"You gotta remember. The way you're feeling now . . . the way I can tell you're feeling. That ain't gonna last. And when it's done with you'll think in a different way. You gotta be careful."

"I was careful."

"I wonder," Hock said. "You even give a fuck?"

I didn't bother answering. Hock looked out at the snow. He seemed angry at first, but his expression softened gradually. The snow melted near the edge of the bays and there were puddles in the low points. Hock wasn't anyone to give lectures. He just crossed his arms, motioned with his cigarette.

"It's almost pretty," he said. "The station almost looks pretty."

A gray shape emerged from the station. It was Burnett again. He stood beneath the loading dock, stamping his feet. He bellowed across the empty concrete bay.

"You ready, Frank?"

"Yeah, I'm ready."

"They're askin for you. Wanna know if you're ready."

"I'll be in," I said. "In a minute."

Burnett put his hood back on and went into the snow. We saw the door to the station open, a momentary flash of warm light, and then it swung shut. Hock tossed his cigarette into a puddle. He talked without looking at me.

"That other thing," he said. "It's coming."

"That's what you said."

"You in?"

I only hesitated a moment.

"Sure."

"You understand what I'm asking?"

"Yeah."

"Humor me. Tell me. What am I asking?"

"You wanna know if I'm serious about it. I'm saying I am. I understand what you're asking. I'm acknowledging that. I'm agreeing. I'm in."

Hock looked like he wanted to say something more, but didn't know how. After a moment he said, "Is it that you need money? Is that why you're in?"

"No."

"You hoping . . . what? To take a vacation? Buy something?"

"No."

"Why then?"

I shrugged.

"Why the fuck not?"

I could see this answer bothered him. He wanted me to give him a real reason. He wanted to understand. It would make it easier for him to trust me.

"Frank," he said. "You're a very strange person."

34

Footsteps approached and then Emily stood in the doorway of her bedroom with Myra behind her. I waved from the futon where I was looking at contact sheets. Myra scanned the room slowly—clothes everywhere, tapes without cases, shoes, newspapers.

"She cleaned up for you, I guess."

"Yeah yeah."

"Frank doesn't care," she said. "Right, Frank?"

"Right," I said.

"You ready?" Myra asked.

"I guess I better be."

The three of us walked to the street, got a cab, and rode to Coles Gymnasium. While Emily and Myra were in the locker room I studied the tournament draw. There were thirty-two entries, with the national rankings next to the names. Myra's ranking was seventh. Emily's was fifteenth.

I sat up in the wooden stands and watched Myra fence in the first round. She came out, slid her mask on, saluted her opponent, and then systematically, seemingly without effort, dismantled her opponent's game. When she attacked it was quickly. But most often she kept her distance, waiting. Patient, precise, and without overt emotion, she won easily. Afterward Myra sat next to me in the stands and we watched Emily's first bout. On the first exchange Emily attacked, parried, and scored a touch.

"She's better than she was," Myra said. "More in control of herself."

"*More?*"

"Yes," Myra said. "You should've seen her before, Frank."

Though she had a little difficulty at the beginning, Emily won her first round by two points. When she was finished she shook her opponent's hand, then turned and waved to us. Myra seemed genuinely happy for her, which surprised me.

Myra passed through three rounds easily, and so did Emily. Emily's opponent for the semifinals was a lithe Russian woman who'd once been the Soviet Junior Champion. She did not seem very impressed with Emily, and I thought Emily looked nervous. Emily got into position against her and attacked immediately. She lost the first point. She lost the second. On the third Emily lunged desperately, and the Russian twisted, scoring. Emily swatted herself on the head. I could not see her face, but by her jerky movements, by her rigid posture, I could tell she was frightened. She attacked again, and lost another point. Myra ambled over, sat next to me, stretched her feet out placidly, and said, "She's attacking too much. When she's afraid, she gets angry, so she attacks."

"You should tell her that."

"I've told her. Everyone does."

The Russian took her glove off and tied up her hair, calmly disdainful. She got into position. She scored another touch. Systematically, point by point, the Russian tore apart Emily's defenses. The bout was over in seven minutes, with Emily losing fifteen to six. Afterward, Emily stood near some barred windows, holding her mask. She looked frustrated. But, five minutes later, when she walked back, she was cheerful, offhand. The final bout started and we watched it together. Myra won handily, and, as we walked home, Emily said, "She's a great fencer."

"I saw that."

"She always does well. She knows just what to do. Always does the right thing. Never panics. Never ruffled. Never an idiot. Not like me." She said all this with admiration. "You were watching with her. Did she say anything about me?"

"She said you were attacking too much in the last bout."

"She said that?"

"Yes. She said you were scared. And when you get scared you attack."

"Oh, I'm sure she's right about that. I make mistakes." Emily tapped me on the side. "What else did she say?"

"She said you were getting better."

"She said that?"

"Yes."

"Really?"

"Yes."

Emily looked happier than she had all day.

"I am getting better. I'm glad she said so."

I could see she wanted to think this. I wondered if it was true.

35

Hock placed his cup on the hood of the Buick.

"So let's see it, Frank."

"Aw shit," Rogero said.

Geroux raised his cup.

"You better drink up."

There was a new stack of prints in my bag. Hock waited patiently while I selected photographs from the stack. He was my most discerning critic at the station and I wanted to show him the best. I took out a shot of a man with a mouthful of maggots. A close-up of the man's face. A shot of Burnett hovering over the man. And a rookie cop with a hand over his mouth. I placed the four shots in a row on the hood of the Buick. Hock examined them one by one, holding them into the light. He looked at the shot of the cop with the hand over his mouth, eyes wide above it. I decided that was my favorite, too.

Burnett said, "There's your brother."

Norman was walking down 136th Street. It was midnight. I had no idea what he was doing at the hospital so late, but it wasn't surprising. He worked about a hundred hours a week and was always on call. He even volunteered for call. He said it was because he was in debt from medical school and needed the money, but I did not remember him working so much before Dad died. We were deep in the loading bay. Norman would not have seen us if no one said anything.

"Hey, Doc!" Burnett called.

"Don't bring him over here."

"He's your brother," Burnett said. He grinned, turning to the street, and called to him again. Norman changed directions and walked over.

"Hey," he said to Burnett. "Hey, Frank. Hey, guys," he said to Hock, Rogero, and Geroux. No one said anything. They all just looked at him. Hock toasted Norman with his cup.

"Look what your brother did," Burnett said, motioning to the photographs.

"Go ahead," Hock said. "Take a look. That's the real deal."

I wanted Norman to take the shot of the policeman, but Burnett held the close-up of the head covered in maggots. Norman took the print, studied it.

"Whattaya think?" Burnett said.

"I think it's one-note," he said. "I think Frank's got talent, but his pictures are all gratuitous. Purposefully ugly. One-note. I think he could do better."

"Have a fucken drink," Rogero said. "Look at'm then."

Geroux poured a half cupful of 150-proof Jamaican rum and Burnett took the cup and held it out to Norman.

"Drink some of this, Doc."

Everyone was looking at Norman. He took the cup and, without hesitating, downed it in one gulp. They were all impressed.

"Jesus," Geroux said.

"That's the doc I want," Rogero said.

Norman caught my eye.

"I'll see you later, Frank."

"Where you goin, Doc?" Rogero called.

"Emergency surgery," he said, and they all started laughing.

Someone threw a beer can at his back, but in good nature.

"Never seen a doc drink like that," Rogero said after he left.

"Is he a complete asshole or is he the coolest doc in the hospital?" Geroux asked.

"He was a bully growing up," I said.

"A bully. That's too bad," Burnett said. "He pick on you?"

Everyone was laughing. I started laughing, too.

"That just makes me like him," Burnett said. "I was a bully."

"Yeah, I was a bully, too," Rogero said.

Everyone was making jokes. We all kept on drinking. I took the prints and straightened them on the hood. Hock watched me.

"They're good shots," Hock said.

"Ah," I waved a hand, dismissively.

"He may be right about other things. But he's wrong about that."

I didn't say anything. I just put the prints in my pack and zipped it up.

36

There was a view of antennas, pipe chimneys, black water towers, and the East River. The tar on the roof was covered with pebbles. I placed my hand on the little wall and peered over the edge. Six stories down, Emily stepped around the courtyard in her white fencing outfit. She'd strapped one of the heavy pads to a tree trunk and very, very slowly was going through the motions of fencing. Step, knee bending inward, foil moving through the air and catching the white pad, then pulling back. From above, her white figure moving slowly against the dark bricks was beautiful to me. Once she paused in her solitary workout, one hand resting on the trunk of a tree. Some thought passing. Then she started up again. I raised my camera. I watched her for a long time through the viewfinder. I let it fall without taking a picture.

37

A windy January afternoon, that whistling sound at windows, and in the darkroom Emily went through old photographs while I worked on some new ones, explaining what everything was—the enlarger, the photographic paper, the fixer, the wash, the safelight. I explained why I'd crop the prints one way or another, or over- or underexpose, what effect I was going for. Behind me, the whole time, I heard the regular slip slip slip as she went through my old photographs—a three-week-old hanging, a starved baby, a jumper impaled on a fence, the Lenox Avenue speed bump. Once, when I looked back, she was lying with her head propped up on a folded blanket, watching me.

"Why doesn't the red light hurt the paper?" she asked.

"Because of the wavelength. It's weak light. It doesn't cause a reaction."

She nodded. Went back to the photographs. She came across a Polaroid of Hock, Burnett, and me in the loading bay.

"I see your partner," she said.

"Burnett."

"Who's the other?"

"Hock."

"Who?"

"Gil Hock. He's my best friend at the station."

Curly hair, unshaven, wrinkled uniform. He was drunk in the photo.

"I wouldn't think you'd be friends with him. He looks like a thug."

"That's practically a recommendation."

I told her how he solved disputes. Knew how to get around rules. Always had some scheme.

"He's made it easy for me," I said. "He protects me a little."

"Protects?"

"College boy. You know. The others accept me because he does. He likes the pictures. He appreciates them."

I went on with my work. Time passed. Maybe an hour. With no clock, no phone, and sheltered from everything, it was easy to lose track. Occasionally the distant sound of the wind whistled outside. Emily found a Polaroid of Norman and me. He wore a Texas Rangers baseball cap and cowboy boots. I stood beside him, frowning, my hair in my eyes, wearing a thrift-store button-down, ratty jeans, and old, waffle-bottom black shoes. An uncle had taken the photograph. It was from two years before.

"That's your brother?"

"That's him."

She looked closely. His expression was serious, even severe.

"Did you tell him about me?" she asked.

"Not yet."

She dropped her head. I could see she thought this meant something.

"It's not that I'm embarrassed, Emily. I don't tell him anything. We don't get along."

"What's he like?"

"He's kind of bossy. You can see that in the picture. When he was a kid he'd gather everyone together and then do twenty chin-ups or something. Show off for the crowd. Want everyone to clap for him. And when people didn't like him, he'd get pissed off. Now he's the bossy surgeon. Yells at the nurses. They all think he's an asshole. And he hates my pictures."

"I'd like to meet him."

"I'm closer to the people at the station than I am to him. You can meet them."

She frowned and turned away.

"It'd be nice to meet your brother," she said.

38

A cop met us out front. He turned his flashlight on the concrete where four dots of dark blood made the corners of an uneven parallelogram.

"He's gone round back," the cop said.

Burnett and I ducked into a low concrete passageway, following a trail of blood, a penny-sized drop every three feet or so, some of the drops stepped on and smeared with lines across them from the ridged soles of city-issue police shoes.

"Is it a stabbing?" I asked.

"Shooting," he said.

"How is he?"

The cop shrugged.

"Is he breathing?"

"Oh, he's breathing all right," the cop said.

The passageway opened onto a concrete courtyard. There were two cops along a wood fence grown over with some kind of ivy. One of the cops held a small, flat-edged handgun near his waist, and was playing with the safety, pointing it at a square of weedy dirt, the one saying, "You do it like this. *No!* Like this. And don't pull the fucking trigger." Another cop held his flashlight with a raised shoulder, looking into a wallet. Four other cops stood over a scrawny fifteen-year-old Puerto Rican kid wearing only blue jeans and sneakers, crouched against the building, holding his shirt around his left forearm. One of the cops was saying, "You don't remember who did it? No fucking recollection?"

I set my bag down.

"What happened?"

"He's shot."

"Where?"

The cop shrugged.

"How the fuck am I supposed to know? Pretends he don't speak English. Don't understand a word I'm saying, right?" The kid looked at him blankly. The cop turned away and I bent to the kid. "What's wrong?" I asked, and he glanced at the cop before he spoke. "I shot I fucking shot man I shot."

"Where?" I asked.

He held his left arm up to show where his shirt was wound round the forearm, his right hand gripping the shirt in place.

"Is that it?" I asked.

"I shot I shot."

"I understand. Is that the only one? Are you just shot once?"

"I fucking shot."

"Just that once. No others?"

"No no."

Burnett stepped up.

"Well, let's see it," he said.

Burnett unwound the makeshift bandage and held it in his thumb and forefinger, away from his body. There was a small entrance wound on the top of the kid's left forearm. On the underside was a nickel-sized exit wound. The kid held his arm out to show us, terrified.

"Yeah yeah," Burnett said. "So what?"

He tossed the shirt against the building and gave the kid a five-by-ten dressing for his arm. Burnett took a pulse, then stepped back to the cop and said, "What happened?"

"He says he don't know who did it. Don't know nothing. Just standing minding his own business." The cop opened his hand to reveal seven or eight small plastic bags. "How is he?" the cop asked.

Burnett rolled his eyes. "Nothing wrong with him." The cop went on writing. Burnett bent to the kid and said, "Let's go."

"No man no."

"Yeah man yeah. You can walk."

Burnett touched his left shoulder, and the kid screamed in a high-pitched, hysterical voice. A yelp. Everyone turned.

"Jesus," Burnett said. All the others laughed. Burnett gripped the kid beneath his right arm. "You ain't shot in the leg. Come on . . ."

We walked the kid out and sat him in the stretcher and as soon as he was back there, among the hanging IV bags, and the heart monitor, and the oxygen tanks, he started bawling. A sergeant with a silver-flecked mustache came over.

"How is he?" he asked Burnett.

"That's the cleanest, most inconsequential gunshot I've seen in months. Didn't hit nothin. The kid's a fucking twig and it didn't even hit bone."

"What's he crying about?"

"I have no idea."

Burnett stuck his head back in the ambulance where the kid held his arm up to show a bloodstain, not large, in the white trauma dressing.

"I dying? I dying?"

Burnett put on a solemn expression.

"Prepare yourself for death," he said, and stepped out as the kid wailed. The gathered cops practically fell over one another laughing. I was laughing, too. We saw people shot every day. The kid was lucky. We couldn't understand why he was crying. I shut the door and a minute later Burnett got up front.

"Dying man, I'm fucking dying," the kid cried.

"You're fine," I said. "Calm down."

"Dying. I—"

"No, you're not. Be quiet. You're fine."

He went on crying.

"You're not dying. No die. No muerta," I said.

"No muerto."

"Calmate. No muerta. Esta bien."

The kid calmed and Burnett sat up front with his head at an angle, listening. We brought him into the hospital and gave the report and afterward I saw Burnett at the ambulance, talking with Hock. They both turned and looked at me as I passed by.

"Frank," Burnett said.

"Yeah."

"Why'd you tell the kid he wasn't dying?"

"I felt sorry for him."

"For the drug dealer with the handgun? For the kid who pretends he don't know English but can understand me telling him he's dying?" Burnett frowned at me. "He wouldn't feel sorry for you. You know that, don't you?"

"So what?"

"So you ruined a joke."

"He's got a point," Hock said, gesturing with his cigarette.

"I can still feel sorry for him," I said. "Even if he wouldn't feel sorry for me."

This seemed to confirm something for them. Burnett just looked at me. And then Hock and Burnett looked at each other.

39

The courtyard behind Emily's apartment was surrounded by a vine-covered brick wall topped with broken glass embedded in the concrete. The surface of the courtyard was brick, with two trees growing up in circular patches of dirt. Norman stood along the far wall against the leafless vines, waving one of Emily's foils, making it flop elastically.

"I can fence," he said. "Come on, Emily. You scared?"

He'd been there about an hour. Already he was joking with her, playing around. He waved the foil erratically.

"Let's see what you got."

She grabbed her foil, adjusted it in her hand, and faced off against him.

"Guess you better be ready for some whoopass," he said.

"Wow, you're dumb," I said.

Norman held the foil up. Without further warning, he lunged at her. Very calmly, Emily stepped to the side, and, making a twisting motion with her hand, swept the foil, which rose in the air and spun off in an oblong flight. It fell, handle-first, clattering on the pavement. Norman seemed very surprised. He looked at the foil lying there, then snatched it up and said, "En garde," and made a very obvious feint. Emily didn't take the bait at all. He lunged again. She stepped to the other side and did the twisting thing. The foil went sailing into the air again. It struck the top of the wall and fell back.

"Jesus," Norman said. "You weren't kiddin, Frank."

He was glad to play the clown. He wanted Emily to like him. Norman retrieved the foil from coils of vines. He brushed dirt from the handle and Emily held her foil out to me. I looked at Norman to see what he thought.

"Take it, Frank."

"I'll do it," I said.

"Course he'll do it," Norman said to Emily. "This is his big chance."

I took the heavy white pad and the mask. I gripped Emily's foil and faced off against my brother.

"Frank and I do it all the time," Emily said. "He helps me."

"Like I was helping you?" Norman said.

"Like that," I said.

"Well then," Norman said. "En garde."

I got in position. Norman saw that I at least looked like I knew what I was doing. Emily had taught me a few things. After losing his foil twice, Norman wasn't going to make the first move. I lunged in and got him in the belly, the foil bending against the white pad.

"Aw fuck," Norman said.

He came at me. I parried, then went in, scoring another touch.

"Damn," he said. "You're good, Frank."

"He's a natural," Emily said.

He lunged again. I parried. I scored another touch. For fifteen minutes we jumped around each other, stabbing harmlessly into the white pads. Norman got me a few times, but most of the time I got him. We had fun, all three of us. Afterward we walked along East Broadway into Chinatown. We ate at a little restaurant with round tables, free soda, and waiters in black pants and white shirts hurrying back and forth. Norman was fascinated by the fencing. He questioned Emily endlessly.

"So you stand in that crouch? The least amount of your body exposed?"

"That's right," she said. "And from that position you can jump forward and back."

"And it's good exercise?"

Emily touched the top of her legs with her palms.

"It's the thighs," she said. "And the forearm."

She held up her right and left arms. Her right forearm was significantly bigger.

"And the palm," she said, holding her hands face up. "It's hard on that."

A line of yellowed calluses across the base of the fingers, and also on the knuckle of the index finger. I showed Norman my index finger, which had the beginnings of a callus. Norman looked at his own hands, which were soft and white. Surgeon's hands.

"We know who the rookie is," he said.

For an hour he talked good-naturedly, and I had a good time. I was glad we were together. But when Emily went to the bathroom Norman turned to me, and, in a different tone, the older-brother voice, he said, "You gotta be careful with her. You know that, Frank. It'd be easy to forget. You gotta use protection."

"You think I don't know that?"

"I don't think it hurts to say it."

I frowned.

"Don't get sensitive about it," he said.

"I'm not sensitive about it. But you don't have to say it right in the middle of lunch. While we're talking. Like it was even a subject we were discussing."

"Well, don't go crazy cause I mentioned it," he said. "Anyone else does anything and you just sit there like whatever. I say one thing and you go crazy."

"Have some fucking tact, Jesus," I said.

Emily was coming back and we were both quiet. She could see we'd argued, but didn't know about what. Norman turned to her, and, in a completely different tone, went on asking her questions.

"And you teach, Emily?"

"I coach and I compete. I do both."

"Well, I can see you've taught Frank," he said generously, glancing at me. That was an implied apology, but I didn't acknowledge it, and the rest of the meal was awkward. On the way back to her apartment, Norman saw an old sword outside a thrift store—a long, dull blade from Pakistan. He paid ten dollars, then came out gripping the sword with two hands, swinging it around, making high-pitched attack noises like in martial-arts films, saying, "Now I'm ready, now I got you." We all laughed and then his beeper went off. We stopped at a pay phone and when he hung up he said he had to go.

He shook Emily's hand.

"It was good meeting you, Emily."

"It was nice meeting you, Norman."

He said good-bye to me, a little reservedly. Before he left he gave Emily one of his cards, then held a hand up and got in a cab. I didn't like Emily having his card. I was quiet. The two of us walked into her building and up the stairs.

"He's a good guy, Frank."

"He was today."

"He asked a lotta questions."

"That's the way he is."

"I bet he's a good doctor."

"He's good at most things he does and he knows it. It's kind of annoying."

"He talked about your dad a little," she said in a self-consciously casual tone, and I slowed. They'd been alone together before I arrived.

"What'd he say?"

"He talked about how it was. How he acted. He said he got so he just lay there. Wouldn't talk to anyone."

"Did he say he thought I was the same as him?"

"He said that you were the one who took care of him. And that you were the one who found him. That it was in the bathtub."

I didn't say anything.

"He said that you were alone with him, looking at him, for like an hour."

"It wasn't that long."

"And that afterwards you couldn't see any gunshots or anything on the TV. No violence at all. For like six months.

He said you kept getting worse and worse. And then . . . you decided to be a paramedic."

I was silent. She looked at the plank her foot was on. I was holding on to the ridged peak of the newel post.

"Are you mad?"

"I'm not mad," I said. I let go of the newel post and started up the stairs. "He's got a big mouth. And the way he talks about it, I sound like a freak. But I'm not mad at you."

"I think he wanted to talk about it."

"He wanted to blame me," I said. "I was with him when it happened, so he blames me."

"I don't think so, Frank." I was quiet. "Have you talked to him about it?"

"I don't have to. I can see what he thinks," I said.

We walked up one flight in silence. When we neared the top I felt her hand on my back. She said, "It wasn't only about you, Frank. We were talking about everything. About him. About me, too. Did he say anything about me? About me being sick?"

"No," I said. I think she knew I was lying.

40

There were some kids about two hundred yards away, playing a game with thrown sticks in the sandy area near the water, but there was no one else around. The wooden pilings in the harbor were empty, no boats attached, and I noticed they had moss on them at a level higher than the water. We smelled salt. Hock and I saw Burnett leaning against his car at the far end of the parking lot. Hock nodded to him and said quietly, "I didn't wanna bring him in."

"I don't care."

He gave me a look.

"That's why I brought'm in," he said.

Burnett shook our hands, then looked around theatrically and said, "Where the fuck are these guys? I been here a half-hour. I didn't see no one."

"Yeah, well, that's probably the way they wanted it," Hock said.

We walked single-file on a path that went along the river, Hock's wiry figure sliding along first, Burnett and I following. This was in Fort Lee, along the Hudson. It was six o'clock, the sun already behind the palisades, but shining palely on the east side of the river. It was late winter and every once in a while debris floated by. A mud-covered log. A tire. There was a pavilion to our left, and beyond that, the palisades. To our right, the Hudson. The faster current in the middle of the river reflected light. We curved around a rocky point that jutted out, and then the land opened up into a grassy area with large, bare trees and three picnic tables that were dark brown from recent rains. Two men leaned against the nearest table—one was white and lanky, the other was stocky and Hispanic. The white guy had a thin mustache. He wore sunglasses, a North Face jacket, and, beneath that, a sweatshirt with a hood. The Hispanic guy was shorter, dressed in a black leather jacket and wearing a lot of gold jewelry. As we approached, the Hispanic guy stepped out.

"Gil," Hock said to him.

He shook Hock's hand. Hock then shook the white guy's hand.

"These're my boys," Hock said, tilting his head to us.

I kind of looked away. *My boys.* It sounded corny. Burnett stepped up eagerly and shook the Hispanic guy's hand.

"Jack Burnett," he said.

Tiredly, the Hispanic guy turned on Hock.

"We don't need to be tellin our names, do we?"

Burnett looked embarrassed.

"You can call him Jack," Hock said.

"Call me Rivera," the Hispanic guy said.

Burnett reached over and shook the other guy's hand.

"Jones," the white guy said in a bored voice.

I just stood back the whole time. Rivera studied me.

"Guess you don't wanna shake our hands?" he said. By the sound of his voice I could tell he'd grown up in Brooklyn. "What's the deal with this guy?" he said.

"I'll shake your hand."

I stepped over and shook his hand, then I shook the white guy's hand. We were all in a sort of circle. Just the sound of the cold water lapping the rocks at the river's edge. Hock took a piece of paper from his pocket and unfolded it. It was a hand-drawn map of the loading bays at Harlem Hospital. Hock had drawn arrows indicating where the delivery truck would park and where the van would park. He laid it out on the picnic table and we weighted the edges with rocks and an empty beer bottle and we went over the whole thing. Hock thought it would take between five and ten minutes to do the loading and unloading. Rivera put a foot up on the bench and said, "Just so we don't get anybody

bitchin later on, it's Gil who takes care of everything afterward. It's Gil who pays us out." He nodded toward Jones.
"The two of us, we get the flat rate. That's agreed. It's more'n
you two'll be makin." He nodded to Burnett and me. I didn't
say anything. Burnett made a face. Rivera ignored Burnett
and went on talking. "I'm sayin this now, gettin it up front,
cause I don't want any bullshit later on."

Burnett muttered something to himself, then said to
Hock, "Why do they get more?"

Hock began to answer but Rivera answered for him.

"Because we take the risk is why. Because we're the ones
protecting you."

He reached beneath his jacket and took out a black re-
volver.

"Cause we do the hard part," he said. "You two're just
movin a couple boxes."

"Lemme see," Burnett said.

Rivera checked with Jones, who shrugged. Rivera handed
the gun to Burnett. Burnett looked at it critically, then
pointed it off at the water.

"I could do this," he said.

"Yeah? You think?" Jones said.

Hock tapped Burnett with the folded map.

"Don't be playin with that."

Burnett offered the gun to me, but I shook my head.
Burnett gave the gun back to Rivera, who shoved it in his
pants and pulled his jacket over it, straightening the jacket
by putting his hands in the pockets. Jones looked me up and
down.

"What about you? You got something to say?"

"Not to you," I said.

Rivera laughed once and looked away.

"I like the attitude. Might look like a student. But the guy's got an attitude."

Meanwhile, Burnett puffed himself up. He pulled out a four-inch knife. He opened it up, locking the blade. Jones was smiling.

"That how you'll defend yourself?" Jones said.

"Fuckin-a," Burnett said.

With an abrupt motion, he threw the knife at the bench. It struck a bolt on the side and bounced off into the grass. Everyone was laughing. Hock rolled his eyes. Jones clapped sarcastically.

"Impressive," Rivera said.

Burnett retrieved the knife.

"Put that fuckin thing away," Hock said.

"Are we done?" Jones said, totally bored.

"Where'd you get these guys?" Rivera muttered.

Hock frowned at Burnett, then took Jones and Rivera to the side, speaking to them quietly for five minutes. They nodded their heads, and when he was through they seemed somewhat placated. Burnett and I were standing to the side. We didn't talk to each other.

At one point I heard Jones say, "You really sure of these guys?"

"I'm sure."

"Are you sure of him?"

He pointed at me and Hock glanced back a moment. He said something. I don't know what. Before we left we all shook hands. Then the three of us walked back together. As soon as we were out of earshot Hock turned on Burnett and said, "You did a great job, Jack. They loved you."

"Oh, fuck them."

"Really professional. You made me look good."

"I don't give a fuck."

"Just do me a favor. When we see'm again, shut the fuck up."

We walked along the river silently after that. When we got back to the car, Hock said, "It'll be two, three weeks."

"Whenever," Burnett said. "I need the money."

"Yeah yeah. I know. For the kid."

Burnett got into his car and sped away. Hock and I walked across the parking lot together. It was dusk now. The lights on the George Washington Bridge were coming on.

"What'd they think of me?" I asked.

"They thought you were offhand," he said. "Slack." He tilted his head. "That might be good. Might not be. I'm not sure."

"What'd they think of Burnett?"

"They understand Burnett," he said. "They think he's a joker, but they understand him." He looked away. "They don't understand you. Don't understand why you'd do it. I don't, either."

The two of us were standing near the water.

"Is it about your girl? You'll make a little money. You can buy her something. Do something nice for her." He paused. "Is that why you're in? Is it for her?"

"She doesn't care about presents," I said.

"And you don't care about anything. I know that."

A fishing boat passed with its lights on and poles out at angles. Some old guy on deck, feet up on the rails, smoked a pipe. The faint scent of tobacco drifted across the water. The boat passed slowly.

"She's not gonna be around forever," I said.

"You can say that about anyone."

"Particularly about her," I said. I watched the boat sliding by. "And whatever happens after, it doesn't really matter."

Hock stood with his head at an angle, eyeing me.

"That's not too brave," he said.

"I never said it was."

He considered this. Then he put a hand on my shoulder. "Well. Two weeks," he said.

41

She was about my age, maybe a little older. Frizzy reddish hair. Three rings in her left eyebrow and another small ring at the edge of her nose. On top she wore some white T-shirt with a jean jacket over it, no bra or anything, so you could see the exact shape and size of her breasts. She wore a short skirt that showed off her legs. She had narrow hips and wore high black boots with silver zippers that came up almost to her knees. She had a really nice body, but her entire face, forehead, and neck were covered by sores, some of which were open, with a circle of yellowish pus in the middle. She was leaning against an abandoned building in that run-down warehouse area in west Chelsea. It had been a manufacturing and freight-handling district, but the companies had all left the city, and at that time, in the early nineties, it was a vacant, squalid, run-down part of Manhattan. She was the only person on the sidewalk for blocks in either direction. A slight figure against corrugated steel, seeming very small beneath that enormous, smoke-stained building. As I passed I looked at her body and then at her face and then back at her body. I turned the corner and walked down a ways. I stopped and turned and saw she was peering around the corner at me. She pulled her head away. I waited for her to look again but she didn't. I went back and stopped about ten feet down the wall from her. She put a foot up behind her and leaned on her shoulders, making the best of her good features.

"So what'll it be?" she said. "You walked by twice. You want something."

"I wanna take your picture," I said. "A photograph."

"No touching?"

"No."

"Twenty bucks," she said.

"Wow," I said.

"Twenty bucks."

She was pretty brazen to ask for that much. I liked her for that. I reached for my wallet and she shook her head. "Not here." She rolled her shoulders off the wall and I followed her to an abandoned gas station. She checked the street furtively, then slipped under the grate, which was only halfway down. We walked through a dim area of rusting machinery. To the left was a burnt-out office with a sheetless mattress on the floor. Going through a back door, you entered a courtyard formed by a wing of the garage and an abandoned building. A tree grew from a first-floor window. The young woman leaned against the brick wall.

"Here," she said.

I gave her the twenty dollars and she took the bill, held it up to her face with two hands, then shoved it inside her shirt.

"Go ahead." I didn't take the shot. She waited. "What?" she said after a moment. "You want to . . ." Her eyes went toward the office. I shook my head. "Well, that's thirty if you're wondering. Thirty for a—" She pointed toward her mouth. "I don't do the other. I'm sick."

I touched my own face.

"That's Kaposi's?" I asked, and she said it was. She put a hand behind her neck, left the foot propped up, arched her back, stuck her chest out. "Most people would just go on and do whatever. I ain't like that. Anyway, I'm an expert at the . . ." She stuck her tongue out. "People come back for that."

I didn't reach for my camera.

"Now you see me up close, you don't wanna picture," she said.

"My girlfriend's positive," was all I said.

"You're fuckin with me."

"No. I'm not."

"You got the virus?" she asked after a moment.

"No."

"Cause I want a kid. I ain't a bad person. I don't wanna fuck no one else. But I wanna kid." She looked toward the office. "Sometimes, if it's someone I like, I take it outta my mouth." She laughed. "I know how that sounds."

I was just standing there.

"Well, go on. Take my picture. You paid for it."

I took it without even looking through the viewfinder.

"That ain't the real thing," she said. "Go on. Take another."

She put a hand up on her chest. She opened her jacket.

"Go ahead, take one of that."

"Maybe in a minute."

Her hand was up on her chest, moving. It went lower. Something grotesque about that. I felt a little sick.

"Is that what you wanted?" she asked.

"No."

"Whattaya do with'm? You sell'm?"

"I look at them."

"Like you get off on it?"

"Nah, it's just the way I see things."

"And you don't want that?"

"No."

She stopped abruptly.

"Your girlfriend—she look like me?"

"No."

"Not yet, anyway," she said.

"No. Not yet."

"I used to be pretty."

"I can see that," I said.

"Can you?"

"Yes."

She smiled and I took a quick shot. I knew even as I took it that it was a good photograph. Despite everything, she had a really nice smile. Something gentle and almost innocent about it. Against that brick wall, dressed up like she was, with that gaunt, scarred face, some really nice, genuine smile. I was smiling, too.

"Now you're glad you took the picture," she said.

"Yeah."

"Now you're happy."

"You have a nice smile," I said.

I could see she appreciated the compliment.

She leaned against the wall.

"Come here," she said.

She was leaning against the wall with her leg up.

"No. Here, right up to me."

I walked up. I was a little afraid of what she'd do, but all she did was put the bill back in my hand. "Come back when you're positive," she said, and then waved a hand at me, turning away before I did.

42

Outside the double doors, Emily set her fencing bag down gently. Beyond, in the gymnasium, we could hear the squeak of rubber-soled shoes on wood, the murmur of a small crowd, the ding from the judge's bell.

"Are you nervous?" I asked.

"No."

She stood with her hands locked in front, almost as if she were praying.

"Can you beat her?"

"I can," she said. "But I never have."

In her white uniform Emily stood out very brightly in the dim hallway. We heard footsteps. Myra arrived from the locker room with her foils and glove and mask. She stepped over and said, "Good luck."

"Yeah, good luck," Emily said.

They shook hands shyly. Myra tapped my shin with her foil.

"Hey, Frank," she said.

That was all she said, but she said it in a nice way. She went inside and when the doors opened we heard the sounds from the gym come out clearly. The door clacked shut.

"Are you ready?" I asked, and Emily lifted her bag. I held the door for her.

There were two strips set up for the fencing. A judge sat on the near side with a clipboard. I sat in the stands with maybe fifty other people. It was the finals of the tournament. Emily walked to the edge of the gymnasium and faced the wall. She pulled her glove on slowly. She gripped her foil and walked back to where Myra stood waiting. Myra and Emily wished each other luck again. The judge made a mark on her clipboard. They touched each other with their foils to test the Uhlmann scoring boxes, and the bout began.

The difference in styles was obvious from the beginning. Emily jumped and leapt and thrust, while Myra simply clacked here and there with calculation, precision. Myra seemed the better fencer, and I thought Emily didn't have much chance, though she held her own through the early part of the bout. They were tied at one, two, and then at four. At five-five I saw Emily fake a thrust; Myra parried, and Emily went in behind her foil and struck her directly on the chest. It was a beautiful move, and I got up and cheered. Myra pulled her mask off and rolled her eyes, but I could tell that Emily liked it.

The bout went on, and it was very close. At nine-nine Emily parried and thrust at the outset, scoring a touch, but Myra was in motion herself, and instead of arresting her thrust, she accelerated it. Her foil struck Emily's chest solidly, knocking her back. This merited a penalty against Myra. Emily had the wind knocked out of her and had to wait a moment to start up again. On the next exchange the two locked foils, their heads not more than eighteen inches apart. Slowly Myra forced Emily from her. Suddenly, with her left hand, Emily pushed her, not hard, but hard enough to knock her back. This was a penalty in return. And for a moment I saw anger in Emily's movements. I was suspicious that Myra's initial penalty was a purposeful attempt to rattle Emily. I wanted to go to her, to tell her to calm down. But there was nothing I could do. It was the middle of the bout. Emily stood with her back to the crowd, adjusting her glove. When she turned to face the crowd, I saw she'd regained her composure. The bout resumed.

Emily scored a touch on the next exchange, and the next, and the next. One minute later it was fourteen-eleven, Emily ahead. Myra, with a burst of strength, pushed Emily back, back, back, until only the tip of Emily's toe remained in the strip. Then, deftly, Emily parried and went in for a touch, and it was over. Emily had won the tournament. Myra pulled her mask off, shook Emily's hand listlessly, but then smiled, and Emily tapped Myra on the side with her glove. I was on the floor moving toward them. Emily dropped her mask to hug me with two arms and some brightness spread through me, through both of us, and was held there for a moment, like ringing is held in a bell.

43

Burnett lifted the last box and set it inside the back of the truck. He balanced himself by gripping onto the roof, then slipped inside. By the jerky way he moved, by his wide eyes, I could see he was frightened. I walked to the back of the truck and stood at the door. Hock was about thirty yards away, at the mouth of the bays.

"Get in," Burnett hissed from inside the truck.

"Yeah, I'm coming," I said, but I did not get in.

I walked between the two trucks.

"Frank!" Burnett said, but I'd already left him.

Jones was standing at the driver's-side door. He had a gun inside his jacket, pointing at the driver, who was a white guy, about forty years old, with straight blond hair, a blond mustache, and pockmarked skin. There was a crumpled pack of cigarettes on the dashboard. Rivera sat in the passenger seat, a baseball cap pulled over his eyes. He also had a gun, held low. As I neared the open door, I took my camera from my pocket. The guy glanced up fearfully, and before he realized what I was doing, I shot, blinding him— a startled, fearful expression in the photograph. Hock saw the flash and turned. I took another shot of the driver as he held his lips close together, looking away. Through the windshield I saw Hock coming toward me. I felt Jones's hand on my elbow. He tried to draw me away. One more shot with Rivera, out of focus in the background. I leaned in and spoke to the driver: "Now we know who you are. We know you."

I felt Jones's hand loosen. Rivera watched, his eyes sparkling, holding laughter. I stepped between the two trucks and jumped in the back, where Burnett whacked me with a rolled invoice from the shipment. Hock appeared a moment later. He shut the one door and hopped inside. He shut the other door and it was dark. I felt the engine start up, the door up front slam, and we were moving. Hock, Burnett, and I sat among boxes of Dilaudid, liquid morphine, fentanyl, and Valium. Thousands of dollars' worth of class-one narcotics. We were quiet. Burnett pushed his boot against my thigh, but he said nothing. I felt us accelerating on a turn; the light from the tinted windows grew brighter. We were on the Harlem River Drive. I lay against the curved metal of the wheel hub. There were no sirens. Burnett was peering out the little window fearfully. Hock was looking at the boxes, reading the labels, counting them. We were turning onto the bridge, steel supports flickering by the window. Turning off the bridge, we were in New Jersey, driving slowly through Fort Lee. Burnett said, "You're a dumbfuck, Frank." He was the first one to talk. He pushed hard with his heel on my thigh. "Dumbfuck." I just lay back, looking at the sky outside the window. I felt calm, even peaceful. Burnett said, "He's fuckin takin pictures. Whatta you think, Gil?"

"I think we made a lotta money," Hock said. "That's what I think. I think we just made a lotta fuckin money."

Burnett hit the side of the van. He started laughing and then he swore. I could hear them laughing up front, too. The rocking motion of the van eased. The darkly tinted trees slowed outside the window. The van had stopped. The doors in the back opened and the three of us climbed out onto the parking lot near the harbor in Fort Lee. A long thin boat cut up the middle of the river, going toward Albany.

"Two days," Hock said to Burnett. "I'll get you in two days. You too, Frank."

"Dumbfuck," Burnett said to me again, backhanding me on the shoulder, then walking quickly to his car. Jones smiled at Burnett's back.

"You did all right, Frank," Hock said.

"Thanks."

"I wasn't sure you would. But you did."

I glowed with pleasure. Jones stood in front of me, looked me up and down.

"You are one crazy motherfucker," he said.

I could tell it was a compliment.

44

I was in the hallway outside the Scala Gallery. In my back-pack I had all my best photographs mounted in a portfolio. I wandered through the gallery, pretending to look at the prints on the walls, but really just trying to get enough cour-age to hand the portfolio in. I was very conscious of the weight on my shoulder. The Scala always had good photo-graphs, great photographs, even. I was sure everything I'd done was an embarrassment. A sham. Grotesque and per-verse. One-note—just like Norman said. I placed my back-pack on the windowsill and furtively opened the portfolio. I saw the dead kid staring blankly, the old man with maggots— I shut the portfolio. I felt ashamed having it in there. I started for the door. Behind the front desk was a kind-looking woman in her sixties with white hair held back by a red shoe-string. She was watching me the whole time, and as I passed she said, "Do you have something to show?"

"No," I said.

She nodded, and said softly, "Good luck."

I liked her for saying that, but I did not turn the prints in. I walked out quickly and went up to Central Park. It was fifty degrees out and I spent the day in the North Meadow, taking pictures, drinking coffee, and reading a paperback novel in the sunlight.

45

Burnett held a tiny baby boy wrapped in a blue blanket. He cradled the baby with one big arm and waved the other about, gesturing theatrically.

"Named him? Whattaya think? Jack. Of course he's Jack. What a question!"

Hock looked away. He was sick of Burnett talking about his kid. He nodded toward the loading bays. Gently, Burnett placed the kid in his wife's arms, and the three of us stepped across the street and stood behind a pillar near a parked linen truck. Even as we walked over, Burnett said, "So, you got it? Tell me you got it." Then, "Don't be tellin me I came for nothing."

"Yeah, I got it," Hock said.

Hock held two manila envelopes, folded, joined by a rubber band. He took the rubber band off, tossed it to the side, looked at the names on the front, and handed one to me. He tossed the other one to Burnett, who fumbled with the envelope, then tore it open, saying, "It's all there, right? I don't need to be getting pissed off?"

Hock didn't bother answering. Burnett began counting, smiling more and more broadly as he did. I took the envelope, turned it over, then folded it along the crease and put it in my pocket.

"Aren't you gonna count it, Frank?"

"I trust you," I said.

"He trusts me," Hock said to Burnett, who looked too

happy to make a deprecating remark. He was practically dancing around, holding the money in his fist.

"We kicked some ass, didn't we? Kicked some fuckin ass!"

Burnett started back for the car, holding the money. Hock held me there with a look. He didn't say anything at first. Then, after Burnett had gotten some distance away, he said, "Cops were here yesterday."

"Did they talk to you?"

"Nah, they didn't talk to me."

"They have a description?"

"Are you kidding?" Hock was smiling. "The driver practically shit his pants. He's not sayin nothin. And if he did, I got a friend at the three-two house. That's taken care of. Don't worry about it."

"I wasn't worrying," I said.

He nodded toward the envelope.

"Jones and Rivera. They liked you."

"Good."

"They wanna call you again. You up for something like that?"

"Sure."

He was turning a vial of Valium over in his hand, studying it.

"They get you to do something, it's not gonna be like this. Not gonna be a cakewalk. They call you, it's gonna be something they don't wanna do themselves. Know what I mean?" he said. I didn't say anything. "But I see the way you are. You don't give a fuck."

"No. I guess I don't," I said.

I could see Burnett across the street, talking to his wife.

Down the block, Emily came out of the ER entrance. She'd been at the clinic.

"There's Emily," I said.

Hock watched silently.

"So that's her," he said.

"Yeah," I said. "Let's go meet her."

Hock put the vial in his pocket and the two of us caught up with Emily near Burnett's station wagon. Burnett's wife, Evelyn, leaned against the hood of the car, holding her kid.

"Emily, this's Evelyn. Jack's wife."

She held a hand out from the baby.

"This's my partner. Jack Burnett."

They shook hands,

"And that's Jack junior."

"Fuckin-a right!" Burnett bellowed.

Emily peered over the wrapped blanket and stuck a finger out. Burnett murmured something to Evelyn, and she pulled the baby away. She brought the baby to the car, which was double parked. Emily was flustered a moment and then the moment passed. Hock stepped up, holding his hand out.

"Hock," he said. "Gil Hock." He shook Emily's hand. "Frank said you fence. You compete in tournaments."

We talked about fencing while Evelyn strapped the baby in a car seat. A minute later Burnett and Evelyn had driven off. Hock rolled his eyes at the receding car, then said goodbye to us. Emily and I started back toward the subway. As soon as we were out of sight, Emily slowed a little and dropped her head.

"You o.k.?" I asked.

"Yeah I'm o.k.," she said sharply. "Why wouldn't I be?"

46

We walked on a sandy path through tall, straight pines in the Wharton Forest in southern New Jersey. It was a cool day, cloudy, early spring, and there was no one else out there. Emily stopped often to lean against trees, to look up through them. The entire morning we walked slowly, side by side, and hardly spoke a word.

Around noon we came across an abandoned settlement that must have been 150 years old. Emily walked ahead, entering a roofless, moss-covered structure that seemed to have once been a church. Her small dark figure against the ruin, in that green pine stillness. Along an old mill there was a slow-moving stream, the water clear in the shallows but a deep, translucent copper color in the middle. We rested on pine needles, lying with our jackets beneath our heads, feet angling in toward each other. She sat up and watched a leaf, floating on the water, pass slowly, and when it was gone she leaned back and spoke, looking through the green cross-hatch of pine branches.

"There are some people who don't die," she said. "I figured I was one of them. Why wouldn't I be? Now, you know, I'm not so sure."

"Maybe you are," I said, but she shook her head.

"I don't need to get greedy. I'm happy now." She pressed her boot against my thigh. "A lot of people are never happy. Not like this." The wind surged and there was a long hush.

47

A congestive heart failure patient sat upright in his ER bed, chin forward, gasping for air—he was drowning in his own fluids—while three or four of us stood around idly, wondering if they'd intubate. I felt a tap on my shoulder and turned to see an ER intern. He looked me up and down.

"Are you Frank?"

"Yeah."

"Just checking," he said, and walked away. Burnett watched him go.

"What the fuck did he want?"

"Something bad, I'm sure," I said.

"Why you say that?"

"Someone ever do that to you when it was something good?"

"You got a point," Burnett said.

Five minutes later Norman came down, walking in his jerky, self-important way. He gave me the eye and walked past. I went on with my paperwork for a moment, then followed him into an empty isolation room. These are the rooms set aside for people with highly infectious diseases. The doors are sealed and the fans create a vacuum. No one could overhear us in there. Norman drew the curtains, then stood close.

"Lemme see your camera."

"What?"

"Don't fuck with me, Frank."

"I'm not fucking with you. How is that fucking with you?"

I held the camera out to him. When he reached for it, I pulled it away and took a shot of him standing there.

"That's fucking with you," I said.

He snatched the camera from me. Examined it closely. A Canon one-shot with a retractable lens, automatic flash, manual shutter, and adjustable f-stop ability. Scuffed at the edges. No lens cap.

"You heard about the thefts?"

"No."

He gave me a look.

"I was thinking about it. About where it happened. I went walking back there. I found this." He was being very dramatic. He held up a small plastic lens cap. He turned it over in his fingers, then snapped it on my camera. It fit perfectly.

"Good work, detective. I guess that means I did it."

His eyes went wild. He swung with his right and hit me on the side of the mouth. I stumbled against the sink and he came in toward me. He was about four inches taller and sixty pounds heavier. I jabbed with my left but he twisted, dodged, and had me in his grip. He threw me against the wall. I went at him. He had me in his grip again. He threw me. I went at him, then stopped. We stood there, huffing and puffing in that tiny room.

"Not here," he said. "I told you before. Not here."

The camera had fallen. He picked it up and motioned as if he'd throw it against the wall, but he didn't. He tossed it on the counter. I thought of taking a picture of him, but, seeing his eyes, I decided against it. I grabbed my camera, dropped my head, and walked out quickly. The side of my face was red and there was blood on my teeth. I paced about the ER bay. I spit a few times and wiped a finger on my teeth. I was angry. For a minute I thought of going back in, making a real scene. I paced back and forth. Then I walked down to the loading bays. Hock was standing in his usual spot. My mouth was still bleeding and he smiled when he saw me.

"What the fuck happened to you?"

"Norman," I said.

"Yeah, I always wanted a brother," he said.

"He knows about . . ." I nodded across the bay.

Hock registered surprise by getting very quiet and still. His face went blank, and then slowly he brought a hand to his mouth and inhaled on his cigarette, exhaled, then said, "So he really knows?"

"He thinks he does, anyway."

I told him about the Dilaudid and how he'd asked me about it. And then about the lens cap and what had happened inside. When I was finished, Hock said, "Who cares about that?" Then, "What's he think he's gonna do?"

"I don't know that he's gonna do anything about it." I spit. "Other than using it as an excuse to knock me the fuck around."

"We could talk to him."

I was quiet.

"We could make sure he's not doin nothin." Hock went

on smoking. "You could get him back, Frank. I could call the others. Or . . . better not. They might get a little crazy about it. We could get together. You and me and him. Have a little talk." He tossed the cigarette. "This ain't the smokin gun. But we don't wanna mess around, either." He touched his belt. "You wanna hang out? Wait for him? Have a talk?"

I looked away, then said, "Why not?"

"Frank steps to the plate," he said. He did not smile when he said it.

"When'd you want to do this?" I asked, and he said, "When did you think?"

I walked back to the ER and handed in my report, then went out sick for the rest of the night. Hock and I waited outside the loading bays for hours, but there were two shootings that night, and a three-car MVA, and Norman never walked past. At five in the morning I went home and slept for a few hours and met Hock back at the loading bays around eleven, but that afternoon I had something else to do. We never caught up with Norman. I don't know what would have happened if we did.

48

A Dominican guy about my age stood at the window, looking out at a litter-strewn courtyard. It was a small place. Fifteen by fifteen. Sparsely furnished. Just a desk, a phone, an old dresser, and a chair.

"I thought you'd be some fuckup," the Dominican said.

"How you know I'm not?"

"I don't," he said. He turned. "I'm just saying. You don't look like a fuckup."

He was dressed in khakis and a white T-shirt. He spoke without an accent. He leaned against the desk and crossed his arms. I could see a gun wedged in his pants. Beyond the door, loud voices in the outer waiting area.

"They said you wanted something."

"A photograph."

He reached over and gripped the gun.

"Are you high?" he said.

"No."

"You think you'll—"

"It's for myself. It's what I do. You can ask Rivera."

"I don't need to ask Rivera. Who the fuck is Rivera?"

I sat very still. He pulled the gun out and pointed it at me.

"It's not like it matters. Ain't like everyone don't know who I am." He lowered the gun. "Go on," he said.

"Right here?"

"Have I been talking?" he said.

Before he could change his mind, I took a shot of him holding the gun. He stuck the gun beneath his belt. I took that shot, too. He stood against the wall with his arms crossed. I got that. He gripped the handle of the gun at his belt and I took a shot as he pulled it back out. He put the gun back in and I took a shot of his waist. Of his tattooed arms. Of his gold teeth. A profile. When I was finished, I took out my notebook.

"What's your full name?"

He looked at me.

"I just write it beneath the picture. Who it is and what they do. That sort of thing."

"El Jefe," he said proudly. And then he added, "Carabez the Chief. And you gonna write dealer, write that I ain't on welfare, that I support my family, and that I don't welch on deals."

I wrote it just like he said. Then I nodded toward the door.

"How about that other guy?"

"How about what?"

"I wanna shoot him, too."

"Oh, he's gonna love that," Carabez said. He didn't seem happy that I wanted to photograph anyone else. For a moment I thought he'd refuse. Then he opened the door and called into the hallway. "Hey. Shorty. Andale." A muscle-bound guy wearing a white suit with a white tie and white shoes came in. He had a white hat with a black feather in it. "He wants to take your picture."

"He wants what?"

"A picture. Thinks you're pretty."

"I'm a photographer," I said quickly. "I'm shooting the people who run Bradhurst."

The two glanced at each other, smiled.

"Wants some of this," Shorty said, reaching below his waist.

El Jefe nodded to him.

"Let'm," he said.

Shorty made as if he'd take off his hat. Then he left it on and leaned back against that old scuffed door and smiled. I took that shot. He held his hands up in two fists with big rings on each finger. I got that. He reached for his gun, goofing, and made as if to shoot it. I took that. And then with his gun in one hand and the other hand on his hat—a cowboy pose. Then he stepped up and put his arm around Carabez and both grimaced, looking tough. Carabez pushed him away. They acted as if they'd shoot. They both laughed loudly. Five minutes passed, with me taking about fifty pictures. Then Carabez held the door for Shorty, who shook my hand and walked out.

"You ready now?" Carabez said.

I said I was. I must have been smiling.

"Now you're happy," he said.

"They're good shots."

"You carry a gun with that camera?"

"No."

"Well, it's better you don't," he said.

He took a sack from inside his desk. He placed it in front of me. It was heavier than I expected.

"A red Buick," he said. "One Forty-Eighth. This side of the street. There's a guy sittin in it. You hand him that. He hands you something back."

"Should I count it?"

"Don't even look at it. Just bring it back."

I started to walk out and he said, "You ever done this before?"

"No."

He looked away, smiling.

"Well, if it's a cop, don't reach for your belt, don't reach in your pocket, nothin like that. Just keep your hands up. Run. Whatever. But don't reach in your pockets."

I hadn't considered that.

"Will it be a cop?"

"No," Carabez said. "It ain't no cop. I'm just sayin."

He held the door for me. I took the sack and walked out. In the next room I passed Shorty, who was sitting on an old couch with his feet out. He followed me with his gun as I walked past. "Good luck," he said.

As soon as I shut the door, I heard laughter.

49

In the hallway I stopped and looked in the sack. A plastic bag held a smaller brown paper bag. Inside the second bag were two packages wrapped in white paper. They were heavy, each about the size of a large hoagie sandwich. I gripped one, squeezed it, then walked down the hallway, turned on the steps, and sat. After a moment I got up and walked back to the apartment. I'm not doing this bullshit, I thought. I held my hand up to knock, and then I lowered it. I knew what they'd say. Get the fuck out there and do what you said you'd do. I walked back to the stairway. I set the bag on a stair, left it there, and walked halfway down without it. Then I ran back up, retrieved it, and walked down quickly and out through the courtyard past some kids playing basketball, and turned onto the sidewalk. This was on Bradhurst Avenue and 147th Street. Across the street was a narrow, litter-strewn park. The row of buildings along the park were all abandoned, boarded up, with burn marks over many of the windows. Kids hung out in groups on dusty stoops, on benches, on overturned milk crates. There was a teenaged kid across the street, leaning against a tree, watching me. He nodded north, down the block. A hundred feet away I saw a red Buick with flattened tires and a guy in the passenger seat with the window open, his tattooed forearm on the windowsill. As I approached I saw it was a white guy with skinny arms, a mustache, and hair slicked back. He studied me as I walked up. Alert, wary eyes. That's definitely a cop, I thought. I stopped at the corner. I turned back. I could see Carabez and Shorty watching me from a high window, waving for me to go on. I looked back at the guy in the Buick, then started toward him again, reaching in my shirt and taking my camera out. The guy was looking at me with his mouth open when the shutter clicked. Another shot as he bent, his right hand blurred, reaching beneath the dashboard. A third shot as he saw I did not have a gun and he pulled his hand away, his eyes fierce, angry. He glowered at me. I clicked a fourth time, then turned, still holding the sack. I took several steps toward Carabez's building, hesitated, then hurried across the street and went into the park.

Bradhurst Avenue ran right below the rocky spine of Manhattan. Directly to the west there was a narrow park beneath a looming, fifty-foot cliff. A stairway crisscrossed up the cliff to Edgecombe Avenue, which ran along the high point of upper Manhattan. As I climbed the stairs I heard people shouting behind me. Three men sprinted across the park. One of them was Carabez. I could see him holding his belt as he ran. I went up the steps quickly. When I was about halfway up, a heavy-set kid appeared at the top. He crouched with his hands held out, as if guarding a goal.

"Where you goin, asshole?" he said.

The stairway at that point ran along a grassy slope above the cliff. This kid started toward me. I set the bag on a step, swung a leg over the railing, and walked into the grass. The slope was steep and the grass was long, uncut. I could hear the heavyset kid running down the steps behind me. "I got it! I got it!" he yelled. Carabez ran up the steps and grabbed the sack, looked inside, then threw a leg over the railing. I turned up the hill, but there were two other kids coming down the grassy slope. One must have been about fifteen. The other was older, maybe twenty. They both had guns. I turned toward Carabez. He'd gotten over the railing and approached slowly. His eyes were dull and still.

The grassy slope ended at the fifty-foot rock wall that towered over the park. Over the edge, I could see the waving branches of a maple, and beyond that an overgrown baseball diamond, weeds growing up in the tan dirt along the basepaths. A man lay in right field with a jacket over his head, sleeping. Cars went by slowly on the far side of the park. Carabez brushed through the grass behind me. "Frank," he said. I turned. He lowered his gun slightly. "Where you goin, Frank?" He raised the gun again and I jumped out, falling past the tree. There was a moment in the air, much longer than I expected, where I thought how stupid I'd been, how the whole thing was unnecessary, how given another chance . . . and then I was in the warehouse where Emily and I first kissed. I could see those marks in the dust where she'd fenced, see the rusted metal rod she'd used as a foil. She was coming toward me in the blue light. Her hair was wet. Her face turning up toward mine. Outside, I could hear it drizzling.

50

A dream of being chased, of being bound, then much later, soft voices.

". . . self induced. That's what kills me."

"Well, I know they've said the same thing about me."

"He ever talk about it?"

"No."

"Fifteen-twenty on his SATs. He got all As in school. Every class."

"He never said that. I just assumed—"

"Yeah, I know."

"It wasn't until . . ."

"Yeah yeah."

Norman's voice changed positions. He must have been pacing around the bed.

"He was just looking at him. He'd been looking at him for an hour. Obviously he blames himself. Dummy."

I think I must have murmured.

"He hears that. That's what he hears. The only thing he hears."

Emily was very close to me. I could feel her breath on my face.

"He was scared," she said.

A warm hand on my hand.

"He doesn't want to be left again."

I must have murmured.

"Can he hear us?"

"He won't remember. The drugs. He's drugged."

"But he can hear me?"

"He's been moving."

"Frank," she said. "I'm right here, Frank."

51

It was a day later. Emily was bent over my leg, signing the cast with a green marker. She set the marker on the little bedside table. My right leg and right arm were in casts. My head was bandaged. My front teeth were chipped. I had a saline lock in my left arm. They'd taken the heart monitor off. Out the window, it was raining.

"I talked to your friend," she said.

"Who?"

"Gil."

"Hock," I said. Then, "He told you?"

"Yeah. He told me."

I lay there looking away. We'd never talked about why I took pictures of sick people, or what I was doing hanging out with Hock and Burnett. I think she'd known I was up to no good, but she'd never said anything about it. Now that it was out in the open she didn't seem angry. It probably helped that I was lying there in a hospital bed. She felt the ends of my fingers where they came out of the cast, then reached over to my left hand and squeezed.

"I know what it must look like," I said. "Don't think it's on purpose."

"I don't think anything."

"Does Norman know?"

She did not answer right away. I vaguely remembered his voice over me.

"I can just imagine what he's been saying."

"He worked on you for . . . five hours or something. He wouldn't let anyone else touch you. He doesn't care what you did."

"He cares."

"Not in the way you think."

I closed my eyes. When I opened them she was still sitting there. I was glad she was still there. The light outside was dimmer.

"Do you have my things? Do you have the camera?"

"It's broken, Frank."

"And the film?"

"I rewound it by hand."

"In the light?"

"In the dark, Frank. I rewound it in the dark."

I lay back and realized that it hurt to smile.

52

I'd been up for nine or ten hours before Norman came in. While I was unconscious he'd been checking on me all the time, but once I was awake he was afraid to come see me, thinking I'd send him away.

"Well, I was almost doing CPR on you," was the way he greeted me.

"Could've said all your predictions came true."

"Not like I can't say that now," he said.

I began to reply, then didn't bother. I could see he wasn't happy. He eyed me askance, looking at the bruises and casts and dripping IVs, shifting from foot to foot.

"I talked to your friend," he said.

"What friend?"

"The one who's always hanging out."

"Hock?"

"Yeah, I guess that's his name. Hock."

By the way he said his name, I could tell what he thought about him.

"What'd you say?"

"I told him he better get the fuck away."

"That wasn't too smart, Norman."

"I just gotta look at who that comment's coming from."

"What'd he say to you?"

"He didn't say much." Norman puffed himself up. "You ask me, I don't think he'll be coming around here again."

I tried to keep from smiling, and that pissed him off.

"It's not like I don't have other things I could be doing. You want me to go?"

"No," I said. "I'm glad you're here. I want you to stay."

53

The police came the next day and I told them I fell. That I'd been walking in the park and I fell. They knew what had happened, and I don't think they cared much. They probably figured I got what I deserved. They only stayed ten minutes.

Around seven that night, I felt someone grip the cast at my hand. A dull weight.

"You got seven lives left now."

I opened my eyes.

"Hey, Gil," I said.

"It should be worse," he said, looking me over. "You may think you're fucked up. But you're gonna walk outta here."

"Yeah, I know."

"So I don't wanna hear you complainin."

"I haven't been."

He took his cap off and rubbed his forehead with the back of his hand.

"You remember Carabez? The guy you . . ." He made a motion with his fingers as if they were running away.

"Yeah, I remember."

"I was just talkin to him."

"What about?"

"You dumb motherfucker."

"He comin here?"

"He oughtta be."

"Is he?"

Hock kept his head turned.

"White guy off a cliff near his block. Police runnin all over the fuckin place. It's been a lotta trouble already. I wouldn't be goin over there, Frank."

"I wasn't planning on it."

"But he don't see you, he ain't gonna worry about it."

"Thanks," I said.

"You been a big fuckin headache," he said.

I thanked him again. Hock had gotten me a reprieve. I knew it couldn't have come easily. He looked away for a long time.

"So what happened?" he said. "You wanted to steal it?"

"Fuck no."

"You were afraid?"

"I guess I was. I guess that's it."

"Did you want them to kill you?"

"Why'd I want that?"

"Don't treat me like an asshole."

"I didn't know what else to do."

"Bullshit."

"I didn't want that," I said again. "Not at all. Not at the ending."

I think he believed me that last time I said it.

"I talked to your brother," he said.

"Heard you had a nice conversation."

"He ain't too happy with me right now."

"What'd he say?"

Hock shrugged.

"Your brother's got a big mouth."

"I've known that a while."

"And he's got a hot head. But it ain't like I don't know how to deal with a hot head. That's the exact sort of person I know how to deal with."

"You tell'm to fuck off?"

"That's what I didn't do," he said. "Someone like him, he's just gonna escalate to the point of fucking everyone."

I nodded. That was true.

"So I let him blow his top is what I did. Let him feel like he was getting the upper hand. I figured once he'd done that, he was gonna keep his mouth shut."

"Smart," I said.

Hock looked away.

"It was easier than killing him. Not that there wasn't a moment where I wanted to." He looked over his shoulder. I thought he was going to say something more about Norman, but all he said was "You took pictures of Carabez and them?"

"Yeah."

"They get fucked up in the—"

"I think Emily saved them."

"When you get'm, I want a copy," he said. Then, "You owe me, Frank."

"I know I do."

"So get me a fuckin copy."

I said I would and he took a step away.

"Hey," I said. "That guy. The one I was bringing it to. Was he legit?"

"Like I said, Frank, you got seven lives left. They say he was a cop."

Hock held a hand up and walked down the aisle. He paused at the nurses' station to see what was on the counter. Then he walked on past.

54

I was in recovery for twelve weeks and spent most of the time in the darkroom. I only had one good arm, and I could not work quickly, so I worked carefully, meticulously. I got Emily to help me. I showed her how to develop and how to make a contact sheet. I showed her how to enlarge, and later we burnt and dodged and cropped some photographs in different ways. In the slow times we went over the old prints. Some of them I liked, and some of them I thought I liked until I looked at them with her and then changed my mind. We went through all my photographs, and by the time I got my cast off we had a pile of two hundred that I thought were my best.

55

Emily and I came out of the stairway into a wide-open, brightly lit room that seemed to be all windows. There was no furniture. There were tarps over some of the wooden cross-slats and paint rollers and poles in the corners. The windows started at shin height and went to the ceiling. I'd just gotten my cast off and I walked awkwardly, stopping to lean against the wall. I was very weak. Emily ran to the windows.

"Hey! We can see the river."

To the west, and sixty floors down, past the World Trade Center and Battery Park, we could see the Hudson. It was a cool morning in early June, and there was mist on the water. Emily shouldered her bag and we walked back to the stairway, where a workman in a white jumpsuit came out, carrying a bucket of primer in one hand and a coffee in the other. We went past him and up two more flights to a door that opened onto the roof. We were afraid to push it because of the alarm, but when we finally did, nothing happened. It wouldn't move. She pushed it harder. Nothing. We put all our weight into it. We couldn't open it. We walked back down to the painters' floor. There were three other men in paint-spattered jeans and overalls standing in a group with their coffee cups at an open windowsill. Emily and I walked down one more floor and entered an unrenovated office space—rooms with stacked desks, tottering steel bookcases, and old wooden chairs, all pushed against the walls. There were paint chips on the floor; plaster dust coated every surface. Emily tried the window over the fire escape. It did not open. We tried it together and it resisted, then released all at once, sliding up with a horrible grating sound and a sudden rush of cool air. Car horns and the undifferentiated hum of the city wafted in. Emily leaned out, looked up, then glanced back at me.

"You want to?"

"I said I did."

"Well . . ."

She lifted her bag out the window, sat on the ledge, then swung her feet around. Gripping the frame for balance, she set her feet firmly on the fire escape. I heard her clambering above me. I kneeled on the windowsill, crawled out slowly, found the railing with one hand, and pulled myself upright. Sixty floors below was a mosaic of oilstains, faded crosswalks, and patchy concrete. Emily leaned way over the edge above me, waving. I gripped the railing with two hands as I walked. We climbed past the windows on the floor where the painters were and arrived at a green ladder. Emily slid her hands into the cuffs of her jacket, and, using them as protection, hurried up the rusting ladder, stopping to yell down to me. She was not afraid at all. I went up step by step, not daring to look down. Up top, the crossbars ended and the railings curved over the edge onto a pebble-and-tar roof. When I arrived on the roof, Emily was already on the west end, one foot on the raised concrete lip. She turned and ran back.

"Hey, it's pretty."

I walked slowly toward her, limping a little. I stayed away from the edge, afraid to get too close. There were some buildings higher than us, but not many. A feeling of openness, of light. Emily came toward me carrying two foils, one of which she dropped at my feet. A moment later, we were sparring. My leg felt stiff and weak, and I was aware of the edge the whole time. Emily did not seem bothered by the height. She seemed to like it. She stood on the little wall a few times, balancing, and then jumping off. We'd been fencing for about fifteen minutes when we heard a banging on the door.

"Well," Emily said. "You ready to get arrested?"

"I guess I better be."

We waited for them to come out, but the door did not open. They shook the door. Shouted out at us. The door did not open. There was one last impotent thud and then nothing. I tried the door myself, but it didn't budge. I think the lock was rusted shut. Emily put the apron and foils in her bag, slung it over her shoulder, and climbed down the ladder to the fire escape. I followed her. As we approached the open window we saw two men in uniform, half-turned, listening to their radios. Emily and I climbed back up and tried the window on that top floor. I banged on the glass, and one of the painters came toward us carrying his coffee cup. He unlocked the window, and with a lurch it opened.

"How'd you get out there?" he asked.

"We flew," Emily said, stepping past him. I followed her; the painter just watched us. He didn't care at all. Two other men with paint rollers glanced over. Emily and I hurried into the stairway. We ran down twenty flights and at the fortieth floor we got onto an elevator filled with men and women in suits. A bicycle messenger with his helmet strapped to a backpack was listening to his Walkman. He looked at us, then looked down. In the lobby a security guard watched us. Emily was ahead of me, carrying the bag on her shoulder.

"Were you just on the roof?" the guard asked.

"What?" she said disdainfully, and kept walking.

A minute later we were in the subway, holding on to each other, laughing. On the ride home Emily sat with the bag at her feet. She seemed pleased, but distant, too, the laughter fading slowly. I didn't understand that.

"Are you disappointed?"

"It's just over with. I always wanted to do that. Now I have."

56

It was springtime when I'd gotten hurt. Now it was summer, ninety degrees out. Hock was in the shade, smoking a cigarette. He nodded to me but did not move from the wall as I approached. I walked over to him and began to reach out with my left hand, but then remembered that I could do it with my right.

"Frank."

"Gil."

"How you doin?"

"Better."

"Let's see," he said, showing his teeth. I smiled, and he bent in and saw where the dentist had put the caps in.

"How's the arm?" he asked.

I held my right arm up to show him. I opened and closed the hand a few times. I swung it around. I raised my leg.

"So you got a vacation out of it."

"Yeah, I got a vacation."

We stood silently.

"Well," I said.

"Yeah."

"I better go in."

I hadn't spoken with any of them for four months. It seemed like a long time since I'd been at the station, and it wasn't just distance in months that I felt. I walked in, saying hello to the people I knew. I signed in and got my radio and walked out to the ambulance. Burnett was waiting for me. He had not come to see me in the hospital and I think he was ashamed of that now. He shook my hand.

"How you doin, Frank?"

"Not bad."

"The arm . . ."

"Yeah, it's fine."

He looked away.

"Heard you had some trouble," he said boisterously.

"Almost."

"What I heard is that you are one dumb motherfucker."

"Well. I guess you heard right."

"I heard you deserved what you got."

"Yep."

He stood there smiling.

"You are one fucked-up partner."

This seemed about the highest compliment he could pay me.

"You ready?" was all I said.

"Yeah, I'm ready."

He got in on his side and I got in on mine. He put the ambulance into drive.

57

A low-ceilinged basement with tossed garbage, broken chairs, and dirty blankets against the wall. A figure shifted in the dim light. Burnett swung his flashlight to illuminate a white guy with brown, crinkly skin. Most of his hair was burnt off, and his smoldering pants lay at his ankles. There was a burnt square below his abdomen in the shape of his belt buckle. Beside him sat his electrician's box, and above him there was a tangle of wire ends. He looked at us silently, grave. Burnett jerked the chair over, but the guy just stared straight ahead, his eyes the only white part on his charred body.

"It ain't gonna help to stand there," Burnett said.

In an eerie, distant voice, the man said, "I been in this business twenty years. I know what voltage I took. It don't matter what I do. I know I'm a dead man."

"Sit," Burnett said.

His burnt skin cracked and flaked like dried frosting when he bent his legs to sit. We strapped him into the chair and carried him out, and once in the light we saw that his right hand was just a blackened nub. His sneakers were melted to his feet. The whole lower part of his right leg was black. He did not seem to be in a lot of pain. Deep third-degree burns kill the nerve endings and are not painful. We got him in the ambulance, lay him in the stretcher, and got a cop to drive. Burnett bent to start an IV, going right through the burn in his arm, finding the live flesh beneath. For a moment I did not do anything. I just looked on. I was looking at my father. Burnett said my name and I came back from far away. I started on the other arm, and as I did I saw the guy's heartbeat on the monitor bouncing around crazily. He gripped me with his one good hand.

"I'm about to die," he said in a small voice.

"We won't let you," Burnett said.

"You don't need to lie," he said. "I know what's happening."

Burnett and I went on quickly—IVs, bandages, monitor, blood pressure. We were only a few minutes from the hospital. As we turned onto 136th Street the guy gripped my hand and said, "I didn't expect to die like this. So fast." His eyes closed and I thought maybe he'd passed out, but then I saw his lips moving and realized he was praying. As we pulled into the hospital his heart stopped. We brought him into the ER, and they were still working on him, kind of off-handedly, when we left. He was dead. Out on the street Burnett said, "You were a little slow back there."

"Yeah, I know."

"How long's it been?"

"Seventeen weeks."

He stood on his heels.

"Well," he said. "Welcome back."

58

The waiting room at the clinic on the first Tuesday of the month, HIV day. All the men and women with bony arms, bony necks, bony knees, open infected sores, hacking coughs that made ratchety sounds in scrawny chests, and weird infections that wouldn't go away. At the beginning, before the medical examinations, there was a half-hour support group pep-talk sort of thing. Emily usually sat in the back, rolling her eyes. But that day she got up, walked forward slowly, and stood in front.

"I'm Emily. I'm twenty-two. I've been positive for four years. When I was first infected, I'd get drunk. Do drugs. I thought when the time came I'd just blow my brains out. Why not? Who cares, right? But I've tried to live a normal life. I'm a fencer. You know, with a sword. Recently I had my best bout ever. I won the tournament. I'm getting better every day. I . . . wanted to share that."

Half-hearted claps and she walked back with her head down.

"Stupid," she said.

"Nah, that was nice."

"I feel like an idiot. Fuck."

But I could see she was glad she'd done it.

A minute later she was getting her vitals taken, blood drawn, a brief physical exam. They sent the labwork immediately, so she got the results before she left. The T-cell count was like a running tab on the illness, and she always told me her results as we walked out. That day she did not.

"What was your count?"

"It was fine," she said.

"What was the number?"

"The same."

She'd always told me the exact number before. As soon as we were back at her apartment, she got her fencing gear and practiced in the courtyard for a long time. She came back in, took a shower, then read in bed. Later that night she told me that her T-cell count, which had always been more than seven hundred, had fallen to two-twenty.

59

A gangly black guy with an afro, a navy tank-top, and discolored skin.

"You do this a lot?" he asked.

"I haven't for a while. I was hurt."

We turned into a space between two buildings and came to a steel barrier twenty feet high, razor-wire on top. I smelled something musty. There was a little door in the steel barrier. He paused, and I said, "I can pay you. How much do you want?"

"You a friend of Gil's, or you just know him?"

"I think he'd say I was a friend."

The man, whose name was Bontecou, paused, began to say I could have it free, then said, "I have a piece of meat in my pocket. Cost two dollars. You can pay for that."

"I'll give you five," I said and gave him the money right there. He took the bill, folded it once, and placed it in his breast pocket. He buttoned the pocket, then opened the steel door and we entered a courtyard with a concrete floor and cages along the sides, stacked one on top of the other. Rabbits pressed their soft noses against wire mesh. Seven or eight cats sprawled in the sun, prowled along the wall, yowled. There was a sandbox in the corner where a shovel, divot down, rested against the wall.

"This is it?" I said.

"Smaller than you expected."

"I didn't expect anything."

"It's the way to be. You aren't disappointed, then."

A hose snaked from the window of an adjacent building. Bontecou saw me looking at it and said, "I don't steal." He turned a knob and water burst forth. He held the hose away from his body. "It's not for me. It's for the animals."

He filled several large bowls with water, drank from the hose, then dropped it and turned the knob. The water slowed to a trickle.

"What happens in winter?"

"I put up plastic, heaters. I can't keep'm all. I have to get rid of some."

The courtyard was formed by the walls of three old brownstones. Behind a door in an abandoned building came various whines and yelps. Bontecou walked to this door, placed his ear to it, then opened it quickly and slipped in-side. I followed him. A hanging bulb lit a tiny concrete-floored room with twenty dogs resting lethargically along the walls, all lumped together, sleeping. The city was in shambles, and animal shelters everywhere were losing fund-ing, filled to capacity. Wandering among the animals, Bon-tecou tapped a dog here or there with the back of his hand, running fingers through fur.

"People know I try harder than the city. I think one of them can make it, I'll let'm go upstate. Into the barrens. I don't mind making the trip. I'm glad to make it."

He came to a large mutt, maybe eighty pounds. Long, dirty fur. Gray hairs around the mouth. Droopy head. The mutt was unsteady on his feet and smelled like urine. Bon-tecou said he'd been sick for weeks, getting worse and worse. He thought he needed dialysis, or a transplant. Bon-tecou gripped his collar and gave him a pull and then the dog came on his own. I stepped into the courtyard, squint-ing. Several other dogs tried to come out, but Bontecou pushed them back with his foot and shut the door. He hung the padlock on the ring without closing it. Scrapes and whines inside. The old dog took a few steps into the bright courtyard and then stood still, blinking.

"Stand in front," Bontecou said. "I don't want him look-ing back at you."

Bontecou took out a lump of wax paper, a little red juice dripping onto his hands.

"I try to get'm out in a week. Ten days. This one's been back there two months. He'd starve upstate," he said.

"You think this is better?"

"I do, yes," he said simply. "Among people he knows. Yeah. That's better."

There was a sort of toolshed with a wooden door. Bontecou reached inside and came out holding a bat. There were nicks along the heavy end. I took a shot with the bat dangling from one gangly arm. Hearing the click, he turned, holding the bat, and I lowered the camera.

"Go on, go on. It's what you're here for."

I moved around for another angle. He unpeeled the wax paper. The old dog's nose twitched.

"I ain't a vet or anything. I don't have medicines. I do what I can."

Laying the bat against the fence, he opened the paper to reveal a lump of red meat. He tossed the meat onto the concrete, then, crumpling the paper, flung it aside. He found the bat with one deft hand. The mutt sniffed along the dust toward the meat. He reached the meat and Bontecou paused to let him taste it. I got a shot of Bontecou swinging and I heard a thud, a cracking sound, like a coconut breaking. He swung again, but he'd gotten him with the first, and he knew he did. Bontecou looked determined in the first photograph and grim in the second. Afterward he bent with two fingers held out. I got that shot. I got a shot of him looking up at me with his hand still on the dog's neck. I took a picture of the dog with the misshapen head, blood coming from the ears. Then I took a picture of Bontecou's face without the dog in it. There were tears on his cheeks. I took another shot of his face. And another. And another. And then I held a sack for him as he lay the dog in gently.

60

Jamaican rum on the hood of a Buick, paper cups, and merengue music. Rogero leaned against the bumper.

"So let's see it, Frank."

"What makes you think I got anything?"

"I know where you been." Rogero cocked his head toward Hock. "You've seen 'm."

"I have."

"Well, what the fuck?"

"Give it up," Burnett said.

"Jesus," Geroux said. "Look at him. He's gettin shy."

"Come on, Frank."

I took out four photographs. I had them all ready—a portrait of Bontecou against the steel door, a blurred shot of him swinging, a shot of his face just afterward, and a photo of Bontecou standing over the sack with the knotted neck, the bat laid out at an angle behind him. I set these four prints on the hood of the Buick, and Geroux, Rogero, and Burnett crowded together, leaned over, and looked at them. Rogero looked only briefly, then said, "So, where's the dog, Frank?"

"In the sack."

"Yeah, I see the sack. Where's him gettin hit? You get that?"

"I got just before. And just after."

"I guess you didn't think we'd wanna see that?"

"I thought it was better without that."

Grinning, Rogero looked at Burnett.

"Did we get G-rated without anyone telling me?"

"This is the family version."

"The new New York," Geroux said.

"We got the old guy crying but we don't got the dog," Rogero said, and Burnett just stood there with his arms crossed, as if he were saying, What'd I tell you?

"Frank," Rogero said.

"What?"

"We ain't kids here. The dead dog's the money shot."

Hock stood back, eyes glazed, holding a cup.

"What do you think?"

He shrugged casually. He was drunk.

"Fuck if I know."

"Come on."

"You're the expert."

"Bring in the fuckin dog," Rogero said.

"Have a drink," Geroux said to me, and held the bottle out.

61

For all that time I was in recovery, and for the first weeks after I returned to work, I labored over a single shot of Carabez and Shorty. Initially I developed the photograph as a wide shot, with the two men relatively small against the stark wall. There was a grittiness and a moodiness to that shot that pleased me. It was the way I would have developed the shot a year before. But my tastes had changed a little, or were changing, and a part of me found the photograph almost melodramatically depressing. I tried to frame it closer so it was only the two men without the stark room around them, without the one bare bulb. Then I went even closer, showing only the heads and torsos. A day passed and I developed the print from the shoulders up, just leaving the two friends with their arms around each other, and not showing anything else. A part of me felt I'd caught the essence of what the photograph was about—two friends together—and stripped away everything unessential: the guns, the stark room. But another part of me felt I'd taken out the most interesting part. Without the room, the guns, or their clothing, it was the sort of thing anyone could have done. It was like Bontecou without the dead dog. I pinned the two versions of the photograph of Carabez and Shorty side-by-side on the corkboard—the one with guns, the one without. I looked at them from time to time but I couldn't decide which I liked better.

62

An A-frame house with a sharply peaked roof, an enormous spruce in front that must have been planted when the house was built, and beyond, through branches, a disjointed white M that seemed to float—the middle of a high school football field.

"When I was a senior I got it on with my boyfriend, Glenn Mackey, listening to the announcer give cheers over the p.a. system. Mom was in the hospital. Probably my best week of high school. The week mom almost died."

Walking away slowly, glancing back at the house one more time, then turning the corner. Lawns, trees, open space, the sound of birds. A different world from Manhattan. I'd never seen Emily's hometown. I'd never even asked about it before.

"Your father lived here?"

"Not for long. Until I was eight."

"You never talk about him."

"I don't remember much. He never came back. He married again. Mom never said anything about him. He was a drinker."

A kiddie park on the right with a sandbox made by four railroad ties in a square, a turtle that sprayed water, rocking plastic ducks and pigs on springs, and a slide that was shinier in the middle from the constant polishing.

"I think she was glad he was gone. She liked it that it was just us. I had these two plastic horses. I used to play with them when she wasn't around. Make up skits. About horse shows. People falling off, suing the owners, everything. I remember, in the eighth grade, I was still playing with them. That's weird."

"I can think of weirder things."

"That was thirteen. Then, at fourteen, it was like a flip in my mind. I started fencing, and I said, Fuck that. Fuck staying home. Home was a depressing place for sick people.

The team did everything together. I didn't care about home after that."

Six gray chains hung three rubber swings. Emily and I sat and rocked and twisted, sometimes bumping against each other.

"I knew she was dying. I just didn't wanna see it. Later, when it finally happened, I was in college. I was only home one day. I practically blew off the funeral. Then, a couple years later, when I found out I was positive, I was like, See what you get? Payback. Now it's your turn."

Bare spots beneath the swings exposing sandy soil. I watched her sneakers twist and cut and tap the swing one way or another.

"So whatever happens with me at the end, it's not like I don't deserve it. Like if you wanna take off or whatever, it's not like I'll blame you."

"Are you worried about that? About me taking off?"

"I'm not worried. It's what I'd do if I were you. What I did to my own mother. So I'm not going to blame you. And anyway, it'd be for the best."

"I don't think so," I said.

"Yeah," she said. "It would."

Two junior high school kids, too big for the spring animals, were rocking them back and forth violently—a ratchety, rhythmic squawking. Beyond that, faintly, they were testing the p.a. system on the football field. One, two, three. Distant crackle of static.

"When I think about it now, when I start to worry about it, I fence, I have a bout. I can pretend I'm a normal person.

But when it really starts to happen, when I'm weak and sick and disgusting, then I think . . . maybe I'm the sort of person who'd just say fuck it. And I wouldn't want to do that to anyone. Particularly to you, Frank. That can't happen to you twice. I'd rather you left."

"Well, I'm not leaving." I was quiet a moment. "Was that what you were doing when I met you? Were you thinking about it?"

She shook her head slowly.

"I was there to see it. I thought it would be ugly. Gruesome. And that it would scare me. That if I saw it I wouldn't want to do it. That's why he unlocked the door."

"Well, that's stupid."

"I don't know."

"That's not going to help."

"Maybe it would."

"Trust me. Seeing something like that is not going to help."

"Yeah," she said stubbornly. "I think it would."

63

Through the small square window in the front door I could see her getting out of the taxi, paying the driver, hurrying toward the stoop. Burnett leaned against the wall in the lobby, smoking a cigarette. The radio rested upright on a windowsill. He held it to his ear, listened a moment, then, turning, gave me a knowing look.

"You've infected her."

"With my perversion."

"Right. With your perversion."

She was coming up the stoop. Burnett was smiling at her. She lowered her eyes.

"You're gonna want these," he said.

He took out a mask and some Vicks. I put the Vicks under my nose, and so did she, and then she put her mask on, and I put my mask on, and Burnett motioned up the stairway with his cigarette.

"It's a good one," he said.

On the third floor, an open door leading to an amazingly cluttered apartment, the home of a hopeless packrat. All the other rooms, including the kitchen and the bathroom, were filled to the ceiling with stacked newspapers, magazines, old clothing, old toys, furniture, sporting equipment. A bedroom packed to the ceiling with rows and rows of cardboard boxes taped shut and labeled—BOOKS, PHOTOS/TESTS, MOTHER'S THINGS/SHEETS—and on to the last bedroom in a narrow aisle between the debris, like a dirt path through high shrubs. The last door in the hallway on the left swung wide to reveal a room completely vacant and spare and sterile, with a bare-wood plank floor and a chair toppled on its side. In the middle of the room a man hung from an electrical cord that was bound to a hook in the ceiling. He'd been hanging for at least three weeks, and his neck was two feet long, his T-shirt stained by some brownish liquid that had run from his mouth and nose, his eyeballs bulging out crazily, and his legs blackened and rotten. All around, on the walls, on the windows, on the body, hundreds of sluggish black flies rose up and swirled as we moved. Buzzed lethargically. I stayed at the door and Emily walked ahead of me, stepping around the body slowly. "Emily," I said, but she waved a hand at me. I said her name again. She was gazing at the body without saying anything, without looking at me. I realized she did not want me there. She wanted to be alone. I leaned off the door and walked out and went down the stairs. Back in the lobby, Burnett stood with the radio near his ear. He glanced up, smiled at me.

"It was a good one, right?"

"Agh, disgusting," I said, and that was all I said, but there must have been a kind of impatience or dismissiveness in the way I said it. His expression changed.

"You're getting soft," he said.

"I'm not getting soft. Just the opposite."

Burnett ran his thumb along the flesh beneath his lower lip.

"I can see it. You're gettin soft."

"Oh, shut the fuck up," I said.

64

Soccer players, age ten to sixty, dressed in blue jeans and cutoffs, ran back and forth across the concrete square in a jumbled mass. The goals were two trash cans spaced six feet apart. A woman with a baby in her lap kept score by placing little white rocks on either end of a stick. I met Emily there every day, at the park, and we watched the soccer players until it got dark. It was fall. A year since we'd met. Dusk now, and she was walking across the square. Myra walked with her, carrying a fencing duffel bag.

"Hey, Frank."

Myra placed the bag at my feet. Emily wiped a hand on her forehead.

"I'm off," Myra said, and as she turned I said, "You forgot your bag."

"That's Emily's," she said.

Myra walked away and Emily put a hand on my knee.

"I quit today," she said.

"What?"

"I can't do it anymore. I'm too weak."

"You had a bad day," I said.

"I've had a bunch of bad days, Frank. It's been coming for a while. I can't do it anymore." She held a hand out. It shook slightly. "I'm too weak."

"Are you sure?"

"Yeah, I'm sure. I can't even carry the bag."

For a moment I saw her like I'd see a patient—skinny, pale, lymph nodes becoming visible, big eyes.

"Well, that doesn't mean anything," I said. I was flustered. "That doesn't matter at all. You don't have to fence. I have money."

"I don't need money. I've arranged everything. I planned on this." She took my hand. "We're all set, Frank."

The soccer players were now wandering about the park, trying to find a fountain that had not been turned off for the winter.

"It's not like I didn't know it was coming," she said.

65

It was five o'clock the next day. I walked into the hospital courtyard, thinking maybe I'd see Norman, but I didn't see him, and I went on to the boiler room, where there were rusting pipes, dangling bulbs, the enormous black boiler, and a deafening mechanical hum. I walked behind the boiler. The pipes must have run beneath the floor, because if you touched the concrete you couldn't hold your hand there for long. It was too hot. The boiler shook the floor. A mop stuck in a wheeled yellow pail rested in the corner and the gray water dimpled with the sound. I closed my eyes. The heat and noise were squeezing me and then I was screaming. I gripped the pail and flung it against the wall. I was screaming. I struck myself on the face and head.

I tried to stop and could not. I tried. Could not. And then I leaned against the wall, bawling, making a hoarse, choking animal sound.

It went on for at least fifteen minutes.

Then the sobs slowed and stopped. I righted the pail and set the two broken pieces of the mop inside. I wiped my eyes and looked out from behind the boiler. No one there. I was thankful for that. I felt like an idiot. I didn't want them to see me freaking out. I looked at my watch. I was late for work. I walked out and stopped at the locker-room doors, and then I went past them and on to the exit. I did not call. I didn't talk to anyone. Fuck it. I was a no-show for work that day. I rode home on the local train, looking at each passenger. After the freakout, a sort of relief, a gentleness inside. I felt close to the people on the train, connected to them, as if we had something in common. It was a way I had not felt for a long time, and there was a certain comfort in this.

66

An abandoned lot across the street from Emily's apartment crowded with the rusting shapes of abandoned vehicles, toppled refrigerators, bent bicycle frames with oval-shaped wheels, chairs with two or three legs, desks, bookshelves, and bedframes. Every type of tossed garbage heaped up in rotting mounds. Shrubs grew here or there, among the garbage, with paths leading to huts made of tarp and wood. By the amount of rusting debris, by the size of the trees of heaven, the weed tree that sprouted in abandoned places in New York, the lot must have been untouched for at least twenty-five years. Emily and I sat on the roof of her building and watched a tractor, a dumptruck, and a crane invade the lot. The tractor nosed into the lot, scooping the rotting mounds of old garbage into the waiting dumptruck, and the crane, which had a jointed arm ending in an enormous metal claw, grasped the trunks of trees with a terrible crunching sound, shook back and forth like a dog on a knotted rope, and uprooted each tree one by one, laying them out in a row. I reached back and touched Emily's knee.

"You ever wish we did more?"

"More of what?"

"Things like normal people do. See plays. Go to the opera. Stuff like that."

"I just like to hang out, Frank."

"I have money. We can do what you want."

She tossed a pistachio shell over the edge.

"Maybe we could go on a vacation," she said.

"Where?"

"Maine," she said matter-of-factly.

"Jesus," I said. "Not the . . . Great Barrier Reef. Or China. Or Norway."

She shook her head.

"I went as a kid to Maine. I liked it."

"You sure?"

"Yeah, I'm sure. It's what I want. I've thought of it before."

"Well, o.k. then," I said. "We'll do it. Maine."

67

The concrete footpath veered from the river and a dirt path went on through waist-high grass. Burnett walked in front. Locust trees arched overhead and through the branches we could see sky, white clouds with dark, flat bottoms. It was late in the day—eight o'clock. A cop stood at the edge of a low bluff. He waved once.

"Down there," he said, pointing. "He's down there."

"How is he?"

The cop turned away.

"You won't be working on him," he said.

We climbed down large white rocks to a flat area along the river that was hidden from the top of the bluff. There was a hut made of two-by-fours, plywood, and blue plastic. I looked in and saw the guy lying on his right side, one arm over his head. He was dead, stiff. I parted the flap to his hut and crawled inside. A neat little home with a hard-packed dirt floor. He was wearing dirtied jeans and a sweatshirt. There was a blue cup near his head and an old two-liter soda bottle filled with water next to the cup. Piled clothes in one corner and in the other a shelf made with two planks of wood and stacked bricks. On the shelf there were a few books, pots and pans, a can of black beans, and a can of corn. A half-loaf of bread in a plastic sack with the top knotted. A calendar hung on a nail that was turned to the correct month—August. The guy had lived all alone in this little hut in the middle of New York City. He didn't look so old. Forty. Maybe forty-five. I touched his neck and looked at his silent, gray, gaping mouth. Outside, Burnett stirred some ashes with his foot.

"You're not gonna believe this, Frank. There's bones in here. Bones and feathers. The guy's been cooking pigeons and eating em." He laughed out loud. "Fuck me. Eating pigeons. What's that called? Squab? Is that—"

The second cop stood at the top of the bluff, his notepad open, waiting. I stuck my head out and yelled to him.

"Eight-ten," I said.

He wrote the pronouncement time down, waved to me, then stepped out of sight.

Burnett stood in the ashes.

"You see any needles in there?"

"No."

"Pipe?"

"No."

"Some guy livin out here, gotta be a fuckin junkie," he said.

I didn't say anything. I climbed out of the hut and sat up on the rocks while Burnett poked around inside. There were boats going by in the middle of the river. The lighthouse beneath the bridge was turned on and glowed palely in the fading light. It was quiet. A minute passed. I saw Burnett part the doorway, peering into the hut.

"Jesus Christ, Frank. You oughtta take a picture."

"Nah."

"This's the kind of thing'd make a good picture," he said.

It was the sort of thing I would have photographed before. Burnett kicked at the dead man's leg. Muttered to himself. I thought maybe I would take a picture, and then this impulse turned into revulsion. Burnett stepped toward me. I must have looked funny.

"You feelin all right, Frank?"

"I'm quitting," I said simply.

"What?"

"I'm quitting."

He seemed to consider this.

"Just like that."

"Yeah. Just like that. I can't do it anymore."

"Why not?"

"I guess I can't take it."

"Ah," he said, as if he understood, and was even pleased with himself for predicting it. "I told you, Frank. I knew it. You've gotten soft."

As we walked back to the ambulance, he looked at me closely to see if I was serious, and he saw that I was. We put ourselves out of service and drove back to the station. I walked into the lieutenant's room and set my radio and drugs on the desk, and told them that I'd had enough. There was pleasure in doing this, even bravado, though it wasn't so unusual. It happened from time to time. People just walked in and said that was it. I shook everyone's hand and they all said I was lucky, getting out, that they envied me, and I felt a little ashamed, as if I was betraying them. A part of me felt that I did not deserve to escape, but another part knew I was ready to go. Burnett and I walked to the locker room together.

"So, what'll you do now," he asked as I emptied my locker. "Follow your brother? Go to med school?"

"I doubt it."

"What then?"

"Spend time with Emily."

"Live on bread and water, I guess."

"I got money saved."

"How much?"

"Five thousand dollars."

"You're an idiot."

"I know."

"When that runs out, what'll you do?"

"I don't know. I'll live a different sort of life."

"Well, I'm glad, Frank."

I was surprised he said that.

"You could do something else. The only reason why any of us're here is because we have to be. Because we have no choice."

I was going through my locker, taking the most important things. I left the uniform, the boots. Burnett was standing there with his arms crossed. He reached out and shook my hand vigorously.

"You were a lotta fuckin trouble, Frank. But you kept it interesting. Good luck."

"Good luck to you."

There was no pretense of exchanging numbers. We knew we would not keep in touch. I put my bag on my shoulder and walked to the door. I glanced back. He was checking his watch against the time on the clock. One bare bulb lit the aisle of lockers and Burnett's shadow was large and distorted against the far wall.

68

Emily and I were north of Portsmouth in a rented car when we picked up two hitchhikers standing beneath a viaduct—Mexicans on their way to Bangor. One was skinny and talkative, leaning forward with his arm over the front seat, the other was big boned and muscular. He hardly said a word. He'd just gotten out of prison.

"Two years," the smaller one said. "Two fuckin years. Wasn't even his wife." The bigger one bristled. The little guy was quiet for a moment, then said in a gentler voice, "Come on, you gotta admit it was stupid. Two whole years. Not even your wife. All because he stuck his pinga in her."

The bigger one looked over at us.

"I didn't kill him," he said.

"Just almost did," the other said. "Right? All because—"

The bigger one looked over sharply. The little one started on a different tack.

"Was it worth it? Could it've been worth it?"

"Yeah. It was," the bigger one said, not turning, and just kept looking out the window. We dropped them off in Bangor and kept north and near the border we turned onto an old logging road. There were pines on either side, and a stream that we could not see but that we could hear running through trees on the left. Sometimes at the crests of hills, looking to the east, we saw the blue line of the ocean. The road ended in a clearing on a grassy hill and I drove the car right onto the field. We could hear the tall grass scraping the bottom of the car. There was an abandoned horse-drawn plow nearby but no other cars. Balsam firs lined the clearing. It was twenty degrees cooler than in New York. Emily picked a two-foot blade of grass and sat on the old plow. I walked away from the car and lay in the grass and looked at the sky. It felt good to be out of the city. It felt good not to have a job, to be able to do whatever I wanted. It had been two years since I'd been out of Manhattan for more than a day. I'd gotten the job straight out of college, and before that I'd been taking care of my father whenever he was sick. It seemed like I'd been a kid when I'd last felt that sort of comfort and freedom, and it made me a little sad to feel it. Like making a discovery of something too late. I could have brought Emily out here while she was still healthy, I thought. But she didn't seem to mind.

"Should we have lived in a place like this?" she asked.

"We still can," I said.

"Don't lie to me, Frank. If I had longer maybe I would. It seems obvious this is better. But it feels empty to me. I don't know why. Is beauty empty? Is there something hollow about prettiness?"

"I don't know."

"I feel something hollow," she said.

The sun got lower. We stuffed our sleeping bags and some dry food and water into the backpack and hiked in through spruce, pine, and fir trees. We were in a small state park and the ocean was less than an hour away. As we got closer to the water the air grew colder, and when we heard the sound of surf we stopped and I stretched out our sleeping bag. We both lay down with the smell of needles and salt and the faint sound of waves. The sun lowered slowly, and we lay there among the tall straight trees, which rocked separately in the wind, and hushed way up. The ground was thick with pine needles, and in all that world of green, copper, and reddish-brown bark our bodies were the only white things to see. She kept her eyes open looking at me the whole time.

Afterward we lay side by side with the trees stretching above us, the slanting yellow light. The sound of the ocean was faint. Emily had a long blade of grass in her teeth, looking up with one hand beneath her head.

"This is how you should remember me."

"It's not like you aren't going to be around awhile."

The grass twitched in the corner of her mouth. She didn't bother denying it. She just lay there, looking up.

"Are you afraid?"

"Yeah," she said. "I'm afraid."

"I am, too," I said.

"It's easier together," she said. "At least I know someone's going to care."

We walked down to the beach in the dusky light. We lay in the same sleeping bag with the huge waves pounding the rocky beach. We could see the white of the surf, and very clearly hear the foam sizzling as it rushed onto the shore. I slept for only four or five hours but when I woke it was already the gray light of dawn. Mist was coming off the water. The sleeping bag was covered with dew. There were little droplets on Emily's hair. I sat up. Emily was breathing very slightly. I watched her for a long time and then I got up and walked to the shore. You could see four or five lines of waves at any one time, all coming in parallel to one another. Gray water on gray rocks. I walked alone along the rocky beach for an hour and when I came back the sleeping bag was empty. I saw Emily from a half-mile away. She was walking down the beach slowly, holding her shoes. We met near the sodden ashes of a dead fire, one log washed up several feet. Emily was shivering. She walked past me, then turned and came up next to me, leaned into me.

"We have to go back," she said.

"We just left."

"I wanted to see this one more time. To be here. Now I've had that. It's time for me to go home."

We walked slowly back to camp, and slowly we packed. I carried everything we'd brought, but as we wound our way up the cliff we had to stop three times until Emily stopped coughing.

69

Enormous chunks of crumbling concrete, rusting tire rails, spikes, cable, white gravel, toppled fences, weeds. It was two weeks later and Emily and I were on the Brooklyn side of the East River in a squalid area of abandoned warehouses and old factories and shipyards in disrepair. I was trying to take photographs in a new way, with a gentler tone. Something I had not done before. As we walked, we saw a man with a beard carrying a brown cardboard box, which he tilted toward us. Twenty green turtles scrabbled at its smooth edges with dry claws. The man spoke with a Russian accent.

"You want one maybe? Wanna turtle?"

I shook my head.

"Can I take a picture?"

"Ah, why not?"

I took a close-up of the turtles layered over one another, crawling over each other. I took a shot of the Russian with his dark beard and the windbreaker unzipped, standing with that box along the river. We walked on and I took a picture of rusting cable with weeds grown around it. Three gutted fish spread out on an old railroad tie, a clump of dried worms, and a curved hook stuck into the oily wood. A photograph of a man with a white bucket in one hand and a fishing pole in the other. The man with his son. The son looking in the bucket, reaching in. I was discontent with all of these photographs. Something sentimental, soft about them. It did not feel true to me. Emily put a hand on my shoulder. I put an arm around her. We stopped and she rested on a railroad tie that made a little bench in the weeds. She could see how I felt.

"Take a picture of me," she said.

I'd taken very few pictures of her, and none when she wasn't in her fencing gear. I said I'd try. I took several steps away. I looked at her through the viewfinder but I couldn't take a portrait like that. It was too close. I walked twenty feet away. I looked through the viewfinder again. I couldn't do it. I turned and walked far away so she was just a tiny white figure lost among the weeds and rusting machinery. I looked for a long time, judging how I felt about it. I clicked.

70

I went into the station and signed the termination papers and got my last check, and as I was leaving I saw Hock in the loading bay, feeling his pockets for a cigarette.

"Frank," he called. "Get the fuck over here."

It had been two months since I'd quit. I shook his hand. He seemed happy to see me.

"So you're back?" he said.

"For my last check."

"You signed the papers?"

"I just did."

"So now you're sittin home, relaxin, living the good life."

"Something like that."

"You see Burnett in there?"

"Fuck no."

"You're lucky. He's collecting."

"For what?"

"Whatta you think? The kid. Christening or baptism or I don't know what. Every week it's some new fuckin thing. Asshole," he said, but he smiled when he said it. "So you miss it?"

"What?"

"The bus? Hangin out with the boys?"

"No," I said slowly. "I don't."

He nodded. Kept his head turned.

"That's the way to be. I hear these people sayin they couldn't quit. That they'd get bored. Dumbfucks, I think. Why'd you do this except for a paycheck?"

For a moment I was quiet and so was he.

"So you still with the girl?" he asked.

"Yeah, I'm with her."

"Well, I'll give you one thing, Frank. You're either stupid or you got balls."

"Most people think the first."

"How she doin?"

"O.k."

Something about the way I said it made him look at me.

"She sick?"

"She's getting skinny," I said.

"How much she weigh?"

"About ninety."

His face got hard, impatient.

"Well, it ain't like you didn't see this comin, Frank. That's all I gotta say. I don't see you got any right to start cryin bout it now."

"I'm not crying."

"I know you ain't. I'm just sayin. You saw this comin."

Hock threw his cigarette to the side. Immediately he began feeling for another one. An ambulance passed in front of us, silently, but with the lights on.

"You still takin pictures?"

"Not too much."

"Do me a favor?" he said. "Take a picture of her."

"I tried that."

"Yeah, well, try again."

"I'm not good at taking pictures of people I know."

"Are you gonna try?"

"They always turn out corny."

He looked at me like he was pissed off.

"I don't know if I could do it," I said.

"Are you gonna fuckin give me a headache?"

"I'm just not sure I can do it."

"Trust me, Frank. I saw what you did with people on the ambulance who you were with for ten minutes. I hate to think what you can do with her."

I must have still looked reluctant. He said, "We gonna sit here arguing about it or are you gonna try?"

"I'll try," I said.

"Do what you can and send me a copy."

I said I would. He put a hand on my shoulder.

"Whatever it is, I know it ain't gonna be boring."

I walked off. I turned after a minute. I thought of going back and telling him I couldn't do it. From a distance I saw him standing there looking up at the sky between the hospital and the station. I went on and walked down into the subway.

71

When I arrived home, Emily glanced up and said, "You got it?"

She was talking about the check.

"Yeah, I got it."

"You sign the papers?"

"Yes."

She looked at me closely. She saw I was uneasy about something.

"I saw Hock," I said.

"Who?"

"Gil Hock. Guy you saw that day you were at the station."

"What'd he want?"

"He asked for a photograph of you," I said.

I explained how the photography was something between us, and I owed him a favor, but I didn't have to convince her. She wanted me to take a picture of her. She'd wanted it all along. Not for herself. She wanted me to have done it, and to have the picture of her after she was gone.

I bought six or seven rolls of black-and-white and when I returned I found Emily near the back window with the drapes pulled aside and the iron gridwork of the Williamsburg Bridge at mid-distance in the background. It was a cloudy day, with gray, diffuse light. Her arms were as skinny as the handle on a baseball bat. Her face was gaunt, with large, visible lymph nodes. Her teeth looked too big for her mouth. She was wearing dark-blue shorts and a white tank top that had once fit but now hung loosely. She sat on an old wooden chair with a wicker seat. I began taking pictures, of her face, of her hands, of her feet, of the distended veins in her neck, of her bony knees, of her hair. I took a shot of her medicine bottles, of her vitamins, of an emesis basin we kept alongside the bed. A picture of her lying in bed with her eyes closed. With her eyes open. With her looking out the window. And then, finally, a shot of Emily looking directly at the camera, in front of the window, with just a wavy image of the bridge seen through warped glass in the background. In a bubbled portion of the glass, upside-down, there is a tiny reflection of me with the camera. But the photograph is dominated by Emily, and what you see at first is a sickeningly emaciated young woman. Clawed hands cupping each elbow, bony shoulders, a neck with the veins clearly visible, and the head beginning to resemble a skull. But, looking closely, what you notice is her expression, which is not of pain, or of anger, or bitterness, or suffering, but of strength, of dignity, of nobility even. Something that did not surpass the illness but that survived outside it.

. I imagined Hock opening the envelope, the image falling out. If Hock looked at it casually he'd think it was just the kind of photograph I always took. But if he looked closely, like I thought he would, I was sure he'd see it was different from any shot I'd ever taken, even opposite. At its heart, I thought, it was a portrait of something beautiful.

72

In the weeks after I took that initial portrait of Emily I went on and took many, many more. I took photographs in almost every conceivable pose—Emily taking a bath, getting dressed, practicing slowly with a foil in the courtyard, resting in the sunlight, sleeping with her bony head on a large, soft pillow. After I'd taken hundreds of photographs, the two of us worked in the darkroom, making prints of the best shots. We took our time. She helped me. We took out the ten we liked the best. Then we went through my old prints—the pile of two hundred—and we picked ten of these. Stump the cripple, the blind man with the wigs, the prostitute with Kaposi's sarcoma, a few others. We went back over this collection of twenty photographs and spent a long time developing them, arranging them. When we were done we put them into a portfolio.

73

Emily was trying to walk to the top of the Williamsburg Bridge, but she kept stopping, holding on to the railing with her mittens, breathing with a rasping sound.

"It'll snow," she said. "I can smell it."

She tried to walk a little more. She slowed, panting. I turned my back to her.

"I'll carry you."

"Nah."

"Come on, Em. I'll carry you."

She put her arms around my neck. I held her on either side by the thighs with her feet dangling. Several times I had to stop and catch my breath. Then I had her climb back up. At the top, in the very middle, we stood looking out at the East River with the barges going by and the lights just coming on along the FDR. It was four in the afternoon, but getting dark already, the pale yellow sun setting behind the downtown buildings. A low cloud crossed midtown, the FDR, the Brooklyn wharves, and then swept toward us.

"Here it comes. Hey. Snow."

The first wisps rushed by, and then we were in the cloud, it was dark, and it was snowing. The flakes swirled up, stung our faces, and only three arching lights of the bridge were visible. I kept asking her if she wanted to go down but she didn't. I took a shot of her as the storm swept through, her face half-veiled by slanting white lines. We were 150 feet over the river, the white lights on the bridge cable glowing, the groaning foghorns of tugboats caught in the storm sounding below us in the invisible river.

74

The man in the park wore two sweatshirts and a knit cap and a pair of sweatpants beneath his jeans. He wore knit gloves with the fingers cut off and the parts of his fingers I could see were dark, dirty, leathery. He was maybe fifty years old. I watched him gathering cans for five or ten minutes and then I walked over and began helping him, snatching a bottle here, a soda can there, tossing what he wanted into the open mouth of his plastic sack. We both pushed the garbage back into the can and I swept up the area with my foot. We went along Houston Street and up into Tompkins Square, going through all the garbage cans along the way, working together until it got dark. Before I left I took a shot of the man with his sack on his shoulder, several close-ups of his hands, and also a portrait of him holding his open hands on his chest, staring proudly into the camera. Afterward I walked on home through the winter twilight. As I turned onto my block I took a picture of the front of the building with the light on. I walked up and let myself in. Emily was on the couch, bent over. I went into the kitchen and heard coughing. When I came out, I told her about the man with the bottles, about his small, dark hands.

"You took pictures?"

"Yeah."

I told her we'd develop them in the morning.

I made some chicken broth for her and as I did I heard a faint tapping on the windows. It was snowing. I cupped a hand over the glass and peered out into the courtyard. The snow was coming down at an angle, swirling. I walked out to Emily with the cup. That was all she could eat then. Hot broth.

"Take this," I said.

"Nah, I'm not hungry."

"Oh, come on, Em."

"I'll get sick."

"You gotta eat something."

I tipped the spoon and poured the broth onto her tongue. She swallowed. Almost immediately she retched and the broth came back up. It wasn't even a violent motion. Just a small retraction, like a hiccup, and the watery broth was drooling down her chin.

"I'm sorry, Frank."

I put the cup on the table. I waited for her to reach for it. She didn't. After a while I said, "You want to hear a story?"

"That'd be nice."

I read her a short story about two brothers—"Sonny's Blues." It took maybe an hour to read it and through the whole thing she just leaned back, listening. When I was finished she said, "That was a good story, Frank. I liked it."

"What'd you like?"

"I liked the way the one brother thinks about the other."

I put the book on the table next to the cup. We sat there.

She closed her eyes and lay back. She opened them after a while.

"You want to sleep?" I asked her.

"Nah."

"Come to bed."

She seemed ashamed.

"I can't get up, Frank."

"Aw come on."

"I can't. Really. I tried."

"Try again."

She tried but just sort of half-raised and then fell back.

"You got here this morning."

"Well, I can't now. I'm sorry."

"Em."

"I'm really sorry, Frank."

I got up. I walked to the wall and put my head against it. Then I came back. I squatted down and looked at her. She was crying a little and I was crying a little.

"I'm sorry."

"It's not your fault, Em. Jesus."

She kept looking over at the phone. I knew what she was saying, and I even think there was relief in it finally happening. She hadn't been sure she'd be strong enough to make it to that point. Now she had, and there was a kind of letting go. She was ready. I began to get up, but she held me and pulled me in and whispered, "Thank you, Frank, thank you."

"For what?"

"Thank you," she said again.

And then I went to call.

75

There was ice going by in floating clumps on the Hudson. Ice was backed up for a half-mile behind the piers. The icy water slowly rose and filled the hollows in the rocks and then receded and poured out. I was pacing. After an hour I saw Norman coming from way down the long pier. It was a minute or two before he reached me.

"How is she?" he asked me.

"She's dying."

He looked like he wanted to hug me or something, but we never did that.

"You need anything, Frank?"

"I'm o.k."

"They treating you well?"

"They let me stay. They let me do whatever I want. I guess they figure—"

"Are you sleeping?"

"On the chairs."

"You eating?"

"Not too much."

"Take care of yourself. It won't help her if you're sick."

"Yeah, I know. Not that it'd matter," I added.

We walked back to the hospital together. I didn't have anything to say to him, but I was glad he was there. We took the elevator up to the fourteenth floor and walked into the unit. Emily was so much skinnier than when Norman had last seen her. I thought he'd be surprised, but he was a doctor and he hid it well. He shook her hand and talked to her casually about the day we'd fenced together, about the photographs he'd seen. When he was through, he bent down and kissed her cheek and said, "I'll see you when you get better." She held his hand a moment. Then Norman and I walked outside and stood near a window with a view of a concrete courtyard. Birds angling by in the square of sky overhead. He looked really stern, and I thought he was about to say something critical. He reached out and gripped my shoulder and held it for a moment.

"You're doing all right," he said.

I didn't know what to say to that.

"You've stayed with her. You've helped her. You've done a good thing."

"I haven't done anything."

"You're a fuckup, Frank. You're a mess. But you've been good to her. You can be proud of that."

I realized he was complimenting me. That was so outside our normal range of interaction that I didn't know what to say. He saw I was uncomfortable, and after a moment he let his hand slide off. Down the hallway the elevator had opened and closed several times. "You need anything. Medication, money . . ." I told him I was o.k. He shook my hand, then got on the elevator. I was left alone in the hallway.

76

It was a day later, around four o'clock in the afternoon. Emily had been sleeping most of the day but was now awake. They had the monitor on her and two IVs dripping, but she'd taken the oxygen off and she looked very weak.

"You've seen people die?" she asked me.

"Yeah. I've seen it. A lot of times."

"What happens?"

"Nothing happens. They just stop breathing."

"Do you see anything?"

"Like the soul parting? Some shadow rising up?"

"Yeah. That."

"Maybe you have to believe it to see."

"I believe it."

"Do you?"

"Yes. I think I'll keep on living," she said. "I think I'll stay around you. And if you need help, I'll come to you."

I wasn't sure if she was kidding or not. She was mildly sedated and I thought maybe it was the drugs. She closed her eyes and slept for a while and I sat back on the chair. When I glanced over, she was watching me.

"What'll you do after?" she asked me.

"I won't do anything," I said. "I'll probably go back to being the way I was."

"Are you worried about it?"

"I'm not looking forward to it, if that's what you're asking."

"It won't happen," she said.

I lowered my head.

"I was never a very good person. I wasn't before, and I'm not now. I don't even know if I'll be able to take pictures."

"You will."

"Are you sure?"

"Yeah," she said. "I'm not sure of many things. I'm sure of that."

77

For seven days straight I didn't leave the hospital except to take a shower, and sometimes to sleep for an hour or two. Bit by bit Emily improved, and I was wildly, unrealistically optimistic. On the seventh day, Emily was so strong she was able to stand. They'd taken one of the IVs out. She sat on the edge of the bed with her feet dangling.

"Try to stand."

"I'm not sure I can," she said.

"Oh come on."

She put a hand on my shoulder and I put an arm around to catch her. She leaned forward and I felt her shake a little and then she stood. I felt her hand loosen on my shoulder and then I stepped away and she was standing on her own.

"Hey! Hey!" I yelled to the nurses. They all looked up. "She can stand."

The one nurse shook her finger at me. I was yelling in her unit. Emily sat back down, out of breath. Later that afternoon, I wheeled her to the bathroom. I helped her put on some street clothes and a shirt over her gown with a cuff that covered her hospital bracelet. With the IV hidden in her jacket I took her down the elevator and wheeled her outside to a cab. I hung her IV up on the coathook inside the cab. I wheeled the chair back inside the ER bay and then I came back out and sat next to her. She told me where she wanted to go. My face must have dropped.

"You said wherever I want," she said.

I was quiet.

"It'll take a minute," she said. "You aren't backing out now."

We stopped by my apartment and I ran up and got my portfolio and then we drove to the Scala. I sat with the portfolio in my lap. I didn't move. She squeezed my forearm as if to say go on, and I jumped out and ran inside. The same woman was behind the desk, the one who'd held her hair back with a shoestring. She recognized me. I'm sure she did. I gave her the portfolio, and before she could open it I ran back down and jumped in the cab. I'd been gone about two minutes. Not more. Emily was suspicious.

"You hurl it in the door and run?"

"I gave it to her. I put it in her hands. Not that it'll do any good."

"Well, you did it anyway. That's something," she said.

She told the driver to go to the Cloisters. It was rush hour and we fought traffic all the way uptown. I could feel her shivering next to me. The driver turned the heat way up but she kept shivering and I sat her on my lap and held her, wrapping my jacket around her small, frail body.

The Cloisters is on a palisade north of the George Washington Bridge. We parked at the west end, where there was a view of the bridge and the river. The lights were on. It was just getting dark. The driver, who was Pakistani, sat in front reading a real estate textbook. Glancing back at us, he saw Emily's hanging IV bag.

"Are you sick?"

"I'm dying," she said.

"Oh, that's no good," he said. "No good."

He put in a tape of Pakistani music that was discordant. A wailing, nasal voice, rhythmic drums. We were quiet for the whole length of the song, Emily stroking my neck softly, my hair. When it was over the driver leaned back with his arm over the seat.

"You like?"

"Yeah, I liked it," Emily said. "Thanks."

She looked really tired.

I gave the driver my camera and he took a photograph of the two of us, shot through and framed by the square in the thick window that separated the front and back seats. In the photo her hands are linked loosely around my neck, and she is looking up at me. The driver took the picture, then handed me the camera and turned back to the front and she rested her head against my chest. In the window's reflection I watched her eyes close. I nodded to the driver and we started back for the hospital.

78

I wanted to take a last portrait of Emily, but she was all tubes and oxygen masks, red, scabbed skin, sickly emaciation, and bruises from where the needles had been. I did not want to take a picture of those things. I took a whole roll of just her eyes. She was looking at me with the camera and I was looking at her through the viewfinder. Afterward, developing the photographs, I fell asleep in the darkroom and woke up four hours later. I developed a contact sheet and chose the three best. I cropped these three prints so they were just the bridge of the nose to the eyebrows. Then I mounted the rectangular strips, one on top of the other, making a square. I brought the composition to the hospital for Emily to see. She lay there, looking up at me. Her blood pressure was ninety over sixty. Her heart rate was 110 beats a minute.

"That's nice, Frank," she said.

79

Four in the morning. She lay flat with an oxygen mask over her mouth. She opened her eyes slowly and looked up at me. She did not say anything for a while. Then she said, very weakly, "Have you slept?"

"Yeah, I slept," I said.

"I felt you here all night, Frank. You haven't slept."

"I will later."

"Go sleep."

"Nah, I don't want to."

"Frank."

"Yeah."

"Go to sleep. I want to be alone."

She squeezed my hand and nodded and looked away and I walked out past the night nurse and the wheeled cart with the medications on top. I went into the lobby, where the old newspapers were spread out and there were coffee cups on the windowsill. I lay on the plastic couch. It was too small for me, so I put my legs on the armrest and my jacket over my head. I woke an hour and a half later, shivering, with my jacket on the floor. It was dark. I could hear the dinging of the elevators. By the glow of a streetlight out the window I could see it was snowing. I put on my jacket and walked back to the ICU and as I was coming in the night nurse was going out. She passed me, trying not to catch my eye, and I went on to Emily's bed. It was empty. There was no sheet. The name had already been erased from the board and the heart monitor was turned off, blank. I sat on the bed. A nurse stepped past, not looking at me. I sat there for maybe three minutes. Then I got up. A doctor stood when he saw me coming but I didn't hurry. I felt ashamed. I didn't want anyone to see me when he said it. We walked to the window and he had the chart open and he was showing it to me, telling me about it, but I was already walking away, half-blinded. I walked down the stairs, past the security, and out into the street. I did not go back to her apartment again.

• • •

80

It was seven months later, the middle of summer, and it was really warm out, ninety degrees. Through the glass door I saw the benches were all in the sun. Norman had pulled a chair into the shade on the east side. He was in surgical scrubs, sitting back with his feet out, slumped against the bench, a plastic cup near his hand, and an open medical book on the table. He'd started wearing his snakeskin cowboy boots into surgery, slipping the little blue booties over them. When he heard the door open he put the book down and walked over to me. I had my camera bag on my shoulder.

"You ready?"

"I'm ready," I said, and followed him into the hospital.

"Have you met Mr. Holmes?" he asked as we went up.

"I've talked to him on the phone."

"You should meet him."

In the surgical preparation room a portly man in his forties, with graying hair, a reddish nose, and two buck teeth that rested on his bottom lip, lay in bed wearing an open-backed blue gown. He sat when he saw Norman.

"This is my brother."

"Yes. The photographer. I talked to you."

I got a shot of Mr. Holmes sitting up. Of his wife at his side. Of Norman going over the surgery with him. Of them shaking hands. Of him looking at me, smiling nervously. Of him lying back down and looking at the ceiling. I got a long shot of the whole room and the other patients, all of them waiting for surgery. And then I followed Norman into the locker room, where I got a shot of folded scrubs, of blue booties, the masks. I took a shot of the surgeons' names on the lockers, some of them with scrawled nicknames, like professional athletes. In the operating room I took a photograph of the steel bed surrounded by enormous round lights on hinged arms. I got the anesthetized Mr. Holmes with his eyes closed, mouth open, a tube between his lips. I took a shot of the row of scalpels with Mr. Holmes's naked belly in the background. I got the row of monitors, the medical interns watching, eyes wide, the anesthesiologist on his chair. I got Norman holding the scalpel delicately, deftly, in his right hand, the first cut in the abdomen, the blade easily parting the skin, entering into the yellow layer of fat. I got his hands moving swiftly, with precision. I switched to color film. I got the blood suctioned away, the abdomen spread wide open, and the organs, surprisingly, astonishingly, colorful—the purple liver, the green gall bladder, the yellow mesentery, and the milky intestines. I got Norman's dark eyes above his mask. I got his bloody gloves with the scalpel. I got him cutting the mesentery from the intestines, finding the cancer, and removing it. I got the diseased lump of intestine in a steel tray. I got them waiting for the biopsy, a clock in the background. I got the surgical nurse returning with the results. I got Norman sewing the abdomen back up. I got the fresh scar afterward, the scattered, bloody gauze, the mess of used scalpels on a steel tray. I got Mr. Holmes in the recovery room, waking up, groggy, feeling sick, hearing the good news, they'd removed the cancer. Then I walked out to the courtyard. Eight hours had passed and I'd taken twenty rolls of film. It was late afternoon, and I had a feeling of pleased exhaustion. I'd done a good job and I knew it. The prints in the old portfolio had sold. I was pretty sure I'd be able to sell these new ones. I sat on a wooden bench and eventually Norman came down in street clothes.

"You get what you needed?"

"I need one of you," I said. "I was looking through my pictures. I have about five hundred dead bodies. I don't have one portrait of you. You'll let me?"

He agreed immediately, and by the way he agreed I could see he knew I hadn't taken any photographs of him before that day and that it had hurt his feelings.

I thought of putting him in the sun, but the light was too stark. In the corner, in the shade, there was some reflected light. I put him in that gentler shadow. His hair was black. The background was that grainy, whitish concrete.

"Do you still have your mask?"

He said he did.

"Put it on."

"The mask?"

"Yeah, like you're in the OR."

He tied it on and I took a close-up, but that wasn't right. I already had that. I took one with the mask around his neck. Two doctors walked by, laughing, making jokes. Norman smiled, but I didn't pay any attention to them. I just kept on taking photographs, trying to get it right. Norman looked awkward at first, but after a while he loosened up.

"I want it like the way you looked in the OR."

"Ah . . ." he waved his hand.

"Can you look like that? Stern and kind of . . ."

Norman's expression became serious, even a little predatory. He glanced up and I took a shot like that. I took a long shot against the wall and then I let the camera dangle.

"That's good for now," I said.

I took out my notebook.

"I have to ask a few things."

"Oh, so now there's questions."

"Yeah yeah. The interrogation."

He waited. I didn't really know what I wanted to ask him.

"Why'd you become a doctor?" I said.

"I wanted to help people. And I wanted to make a lot of money."

"Honorable."

"You know. It was a good fit."

"And why surgery?"

"I found sick people didn't like me."

"Oh come on."

He spoke matter-of-factly.

"Sick people don't like me. I have no tact. And it bothers them."

I was writing this down.

"Like with Dad. You were the one he wanted to see. When he was sick, depressed, it was you he liked. So I knew that about myself. I grate on sick people. So I went into surgery. Not what I initially intended, but big deal. I make five hundred thousand dollars a year and all my patients are asleep. I don't have to deal with a bunch of people whining. Or not liking me. Or both."

I wrote all this down just as he'd said it. It was the first time I'd heard any of that. I thought of asking more, but he seemed uncomfortable already.

"Are you a good surgeon?"

"I'm a great surgeon," he said.

I wrote that down, too. He was looking at his watch.

"Frank."

"Yeah, I know."

"It's good to see you."

"It's good to see you," I said.

"If you have any questions . . ."

"Yeah yeah. I'll talk to you."

I looked at his feet. He had those blue booties over the snakeskin boots.

"I have to get this," I said.

I bent down and took a shot.

"You realize those boots are ridiculous."

"You think I give a fuck?" he said, and I held a hand up and walked to the doorway. I was thinking about what he'd told me. I was thinking of the studied, casual tone he used when he spoke of our father. I walked back. Norman was gathering his book, his cup. I was going to say something more, tell him that what he'd said wasn't entirely true, that Dad had wanted to see him, but didn't know how to show it, that no one in our family expressed themselves directly. After a moment, it didn't seem necessary to say this. There was time. I'd bring him the developed photographs. We'd look at them together. It would be something between us. We'd talk then. I just nodded to him, turned.

"I'll see you," he said over my shoulder.

I walked back out, holding my camera.

81

It was an hour later. I was on the subway going home. I felt good about the photographs. I felt good about talking to Norman. I imagined telling Emily about these things, and I imagined her response.

As the J train clacked its way up the bridge toward Brooklyn I had a view of the Lower East Side, Houston Street, and Emily's apartment building. I thought of taking a picture out the window, framed by the window. She would have liked that. I held the camera to my eye but the view was cut by a swinging string of lights on a bridge cable. One light in the string flickered, faded, surged, and then died completely. Slightly, almost imperceptibly, the other bulbs brightened.

Acknowledgments

I am indebted to several people who helped with the completion of this book. I want to thank Susan Falls and Tom Garrigus, who each gave specific suggestions at critical moments. I want to thank Tracey Thorne for her expertise on fencing. I want to thank my family for moral support throughout the long process. I want to thank David McCormick and Dan Menaker for believing in the book—it would not be here in this form without them. I want to thank Steve Gaghan for reading it many times, and for his excellent suggestions on plot and character. And last, and particularly, I want to thank my wife, Amy Billone, for her unerring line editing, and her unrelenting optimism.

S A F E L I G H T

Shannon Burke

A Conversation with Shannon Burke

DAVE MAHER

Dave Maher was a paramedic for the New York City Fire Department. Dave and Shannon worked together at Station 18 in Harlem for five years.

Dave Maher: I want you to talk a little bit about how you decided to be a writer.

Shannon Burke: Well, I'd always written things as a kid—poetry and song lyrics, and little plays that I videotaped. Short stories. That sort of thing. In college I was an English major and I guess I wrote stories and some poetry, though I hardly showed anybody. I think I was embarrassed about it. After college I was planning on going to law school, but I wanted to go traveling first. I moved back home for about four months. I worked as a cabdriver and I taught tennis. I saved about ten thousand dollars, then took off for a year, and while I was gone, over that year, I read around a hundred novels: Dostoyevsky, Tolstoy, Flaubert, Dickens, Hemingway, Faulkner, García Márquez, Fielding, George Eliot, Virginia Woolf, everything. And it really was . . . life-changing for me. By the time I came back I'd decided I wanted to be a writer.

DM: And what'd your parents say?

SB: They were really happy.

DM: I detect a little sarcasm.

SB: Uh, yeah. . . . They weren't bad about it. They were even supportive. But I don't think they saw it as a shrewd career decision.

DM: So did you decide to be a paramedic then, as a day job?

SB: No, no. That didn't happen for a long time. I just moved around to different cities and worked shitty jobs for the next five or six years. I was in Chapel Hill for a while, where I'd gone to school. Then I was in Prescott, Arizona. I was in Los Angeles, New Orleans, Chicago. I went to Mexico for about five months at one point.

DM: Was there a design behind the places you went to?

SB: Not really. The first place I went after Chapel Hill was Prescott. I just wanted to live in a small town. I'd never done that before. I was interested in the southwest and my finger sort of fell on Prescott on the map. I thought I'd check it out, but then my car broke down and I sold it to the junkyard, so I got a job at the Pizza Hut and stayed.

DM: And you were by yourself?

SB: Yeah, yeah. It was kind of weird. For that whole time, five or six years, I just moved around by myself. I wrote during the day. I worked at night. I lived in the worst places. Like, in New Orleans for a while I lived in a transients' hotel—the sort of place where homeless people sleep in the hallways. I was the weirdo who was always carrying a book. It was kind of lonely.

DM: And you were writing during this time?

SB: Oh, yeah. All the time. Every day. Initially I wrote stories. I think I wrote about fifty bad stories, one after the other.

DM: And they were based on things you were seeing in these towns?

SB: Not really. It's interesting. I mean, in retrospect it's interesting. These were mostly stories without plots or characters.

DM: That's one way to do it.

SB: That's exactly what everyone else thought, too. My sister once said, "Hey, Shannon, maybe you should write a story where something happens." And of course she was right. But at the time I thought that plot didn't matter. I was obsessed with style. And I just . . . wasn't seeing the big picture. Later on, it might have ended up helping me. I mean, that I spent all that time thinking about the most efficient way of describing something. Or the most pleasing way to have dialogue flow. But it would have been much easier to have gone at it from the other direction. Like, start out thinking about a plot and characters. Because at least then I could have written something that other people wanted to read, even if it wasn't great literature. The way I did it, there might have been a nice sentence or description, but when there's no plot, people are just like, What the hell is this?

DM: To me it sounds like the classic beginning for a lot of people, which is, you want to describe how you feel about a particular event or person, and that gets you started, but you don't know how to put a story together.

SB: Well, that was definitely the case with me. I didn't know how to put a story together. But then, as time went on, I got a little better.

DM: And so when did you decide to become a paramedic?

SB: It was in 1992. I was living in New Orleans at the time, and one night I saw someone murdered. I was working at a bookstore in the French Quarter then, and the

deal was, the bookstore gave the people at the movie theater a ten percent discount, and in return we got to go to
movies for free. And since I was making four-fifty an hour,
the only thing I could do for entertainment was go to the
free movie theater. I didn't have a TV. My only other entertainment was my library card. So I saw all the movies
twice. Anyway, it was maybe one in the morning, and I
was coming back from the movie theater, and I heard
what I thought were firecrackers, and then it was, like,
Oh, that was gunfire. I looked up and maybe . . . fifty feet
away someone was lying in the street, and a guy was walking toward me with a gun. I stopped on the sidewalk. We
looked right at each other. The guy got in a car parked the
wrong way on a one-way street. He drove past me, then
turned the corner, and I ran up the street, and there was
this girl, this woman . . .

DM: How old?

SB: Twenty-seven. She was a tourist. A British fashion
designer. She was out with her fiancé and they'd gotten
mugged or something. The fiancé was just freaking out.
Screaming. Trying to kiss the woman. Trying to wake her
up. I saw that she was shot in the right arm. I used a
T-shirt and tried to wrap up her arm. I remember the
whole thing vividly, way more vividly than I remember,
like, the other hundred gunshot wounds I've seen since
then. She was unconscious and she started vomiting.

And the one thing I knew at that time is that you weren't supposed to move the neck. So the fiancé rolled her body and I held her head and we tilted her so the vomit came out. After I rolled her back I saw there was blood on the hand that had been on her head and I realized she was shot in the head, too. She died later that night. And I definitely . . . I felt guilty. I thought I should have known first aid or something. Like I could have saved her. Now I know better.

DM: Now you realize it would have been hopeless if you were the surgeon general and she was shot on an operating table.

SB: Yeah, exactly. Anyway, I ended up taking an EMT class because of that. And then, right around the time I became an EMT, I broke up with my girlfriend and so I had no reason to be anywhere and I figured I might as well go to New York and work on an ambulance. I figured it would be the most extreme place to do it.

DM: So when you went to New York City you had it already targeted in your mind that you were going to pursue a job in the fire department?

SB: I don't know if it was so clear at the time that I wanted to work for the fire department. I just knew I was going to try to get a job on some ambulance. And I did. I worked for the privates for a year as an EMT, and then I started going to paramedic school. I graduated from medic school in December of 1995. I went on vacation for four weeks to kind of decompress, and when I came back I realized the fire department had opened up for applications, and that I'd almost missed the hiring. By the time I showed up, almost everyone had already applied. I went in on, like, the afternoon of the last day. It was a first-come-first-served type of situation, so all the people applying on the last day were supposed to be called up in two or three years. I went in to hand in my application and the interviewer looked it over and saw that I had a college degree, and that I went to a good school, and I had good grades and all that, and at one point he just said, "What are you doing here? Do you know what it's going to be like?" I said I did and that I wanted the job. After the interview I walked out and then I thought about it, and I walked back in, and I said, "Listen, I don't know what you think, like I shouldn't even be applying, but I really want this job. I've never had a job that paid this well. And I really need this job." Basically, I let him know I was desperate. The interviewer saw I wasn't bullshitting him, and I guess he took pity on me. He took my folder from one pile and put it in another pile and said, "They'll call you within the week." And they did.

DM: I remember that. We were both hired at the same time and sent to Harlem.

SB: I was glad. I requested Harlem. I thought it was the badass station to go to. I was an idiot. I had no idea what I was getting into. You remember how it was?

DM: Oh, yeah, I don't know how we did it.

SB: I remember this one job in the first month. We came into this hallway in Washington Heights. Our patient was this kid who'd been stabbed somewhere in the abdomen, and he'd crawled thirty feet down this hallway. There was a swath of blood about three feet wide. I mean, there was a ton of blood. And so we, like, followed the trail of blood and got to him and turned him over and each of us went to an arm to start an IV, and my partner looked up at me and said, "Just so you know, Shannon, if you miss this IV he'll die."

DM: Oh, God. You gotta love it. The sympathetic veteran medic. Did you get it?

SB: You know what? I did get it. And he missed it.

DM: Oh, that's perfect.

SB: Every day it was like that. Every day some new drama. In those first months I was moved around a lot and I worked with some bad medics. I thought it was normal to get in fights with the patients every day. I thought it was normal to get in screaming arguments with bystanders. It was only later that I saw a lot of the stuff that happened was insane.

DM: Have you written about it?

SB: A little. And of course some of that is reflected in *Safelight*. But a lot of it was so extreme it would be hard to make it believable. I still don't understand why some of those people became paramedics in the first place. Or why they chose to work in Harlem.

DM: But that all goes back to . . . you have to start breaking down the personality paradigm of people who go into EMS. A percentage of the guys are always going to be people who lack self-esteem, so they try to ally themselves or drape themselves in a moral cause so they can feel good about themselves. Why do you think there are so many people in EMS who literally perpetuate the lie about what the job's really like? They'll tell you they're sick of that person and sick of those people and sick of everyone, and that they aren't appreciated and all that, but then, when an outsider comes around asking questions, they'll start talking about some job, about how they did something heroic and lifesaving, and I'm like, What a phony. But it makes sense. They need to perpetuate the lie, because that's how they derive their own sense of importance.

SB: But it's more complicated than it just being a lie, because there *are* life-altering moments. There's a life-or-death job once every two or three weeks.

DM: I don't dispute that. But what I do dispute is people who create a false impression of what we do, tell people it's more dramatic than it is, for self-aggrandizing purposes.

SB: What? Every medic isn't an altruist, just out there helping people?

DM: Yeah, that's the canned line, but you and I both know what the truth is about what happens on the job. And how most of the people are. And how we were ourselves. Everyone puts up some barrier. Which I'm not saying is wrong. I'm saying it's inevitable. But you might as well . . . admit it's there. Anyway, let's get back to you. After you got hired you moved up to Harlem, right?

SB: Not right away. After a few years.

DM: Did you move up there so you could write about it?

SB: Yeah, it was for that. I spent forty hours a week in Harlem on the ambulance, as you know, but once you move up there it's a different story. Living there you realize that for every menace to society there are five hundred regular families just trying to get by. I grew up in the suburbs, and when I got up to Harlem I imagined crack houses and all that. But most of that portrayal is bullshit. It took me a while to realize that it was just a normal working-class neighborhood.

DM: Not even working-class anymore. But I guess when you come from suburbia and go to a place like Harlem you've been conditioned to imagine it's going to be like Beirut. Not that I know anything about Beirut. But you get the point.

SB: Definitely. It's what I thought. And I hope I got beyond that. And though the book isn't really about Harlem, I hope my feeling for what it was like shows through.

DM: I think it does, though I think it also shows some of the grimmer aspects. I mean, poverty and HIV and all that . . . Before you started writing the book, did you know that you were going to write about those things? I mean, did you start with the idea that this is going to be a love story between a paramedic and a girl with HIV?

SB: That is the one idea I started with. Everything else changed, but that love story was the starting point for me, and it stayed in the book through all its incarnations. Maybe it represented the hopelessness of what we saw and lived through. Or the seeming hopelessness, and then trying to make sense of it. Anyway, that was the anchor. And I think it was the only one.

DM: Are the people in *Safelight* supposed to represent actual people at the station?

SB: No.

DM: But you were working as a medic, working with people we both knew. Were you not incorporating real traits of those guys into the story you were trying to tell?

SB: Well, it's a novel. You invent a character, and then the character starts getting bent around and taking on other qualities, and some of those qualities may be recognizable as coming from people you know, but other qualities are complete invention, and you get a mixture of all kinds of things from different places. And then these characters end up doing things that nobody you know would ever do, and so what you end up with is fiction. And that's the way I think of it when I'm writing. I remember the last edits I made on the book. I had to write more scenes. Maybe it was ten scenes. And it was so easy to write them because by that point I knew all the characters intimately. I knew where they lived and what they would say and what they'd been through. So I'd just sit down and write the scenes without revision. It was a reminder of how much of writing is actually thinking and getting things clear in your head, that the writing part is just the final result. That so much of it is preparation.

DM: That kind of gets at something else. I know how you write. You outline obsessively. You work out every possibility in your mind before you're ready to write.

SB: Yeah, I do. The problem with writing in that spare style is that if there's any flaw it's really obvious. Verbosity tends to cover over or wash out structural problems, and even character problems, and so you can get away with some things you couldn't get away with in a book with a spare style. So I had to think about the structure and the shape of the book a lot before I started. But when I finally got down to writing I didn't look at the outline. Because I didn't want to know exactly what was there. I didn't want to be following it like a connect-the-dots sort of thing. I just wanted to have a general idea and then let the thing move forward on its own, but within the confines, hopefully, of what I'd planned out before. So, it's a give-and-take. You have to be constrained to some extent, but you have to leave yourself room for inspiration.

DM: Were there writers you were inspired by?

SB: Well, sure. Everyone's inspired by someone. And anyone that's minimalist is always said to be inspired by Hemingway. And I don't deny it. I really admired Hemingway when I was young. And I still admire him. *The Sun Also Rises* is one of my favorite books. But I don't think it's as simple as only being influenced by Hemingway. There's Knut Hamsun, James Kelman, Coetzee, Tolstoy, Turgenev, Kawabata. A bunch of people. And if you look at all those people, you'll see they all wrote fairly succinct, emotional stories. Obviously not all of Tolstoy was succinct. Or even Kelman or Hamsun. But they all did write in that spare, emotional style at some point. And that's what I was drawn to. Oh, and also all those French books. Remember I used to read all those French books on the ambulance?

DM: Yeah. In French.

SB: Right. Well, around the time I was writing *Safelight* I was reading Flaubert, *Les Misérables,* and a bunch of Zola, and I remember learning something from all that, particularly from the Zola. In Zola you have the heroes doing horrible things. It's like the heroes are raping fourteen-year-old virgins. And I realized that as long as the situation was bad enough, you could have the main character do almost anything and you'd forgive him. You'd just say he was a good person in a bad circumstance. And that lesson was really important for me when I was writing *Safelight*. It gave me confidence to do what I wanted to, to really show the brutality and also the mundaneness of the job. And the total disaffection of everyone up there.

DM: Well, that disaffected tone is definitely, for me, one of the best parts of the book. Because it's so real. I mean, what really got to me about the job was not so much the gruesome aspects of it, but the repetition. And the boredom. And just . . . the weirdness. You don't see that on, like, the TV shows. I mean, the weirdness and the irony just happened on all levels. Like I remember one time I worked on a cardiac arrest in front of a Christmas tree with all the family sitting there, like, half the presents unwrapped.

SB: Do you remember the job that Scott had with the Christmas tree? There were four people in the apartment, and they were doing the candles-on-the-Christmas-tree thing. So the Christmas tree catches on fire and the father tried to be heroic. He grabbed the burning tree to pull it out of the apartment. He made it all the way to the front door, then collapsed out in the hallway. The father ended up living because he was out in the hallway. But everyone else was trapped. The burning tree was blocking the only exit and the fire had spread across the whole apartment. The windows had bars on them. The mother and the two kids died.

DM: Oh, God. That's horrible. I had a few like that, where . . . you just can't imagine how bad it was. I remember we had one where a girl had drowned, and all the mother seemed to care about was convincing us she'd had nothing to do with it. The mother kept pulling out this store receipt with the time on it, to prove she wasn't in the apartment when the daughter died. I swear, she kept showing us this receipt. And we're all just sitting there, doing CPR on her daughter, while she's holding up this receipt. I'm like, I can't even tell anyone this story. It's all too weird. And half the time the other medics didn't even want to talk about it.

SB: I know I didn't. Not the real stuff, anyway.

DM: Well, that's exactly the way it is. And getting back to your book, that's definitely the way your main character was. Would you say Frank was based on yourself? Is he you? Is he a part of you?

SB: Well, he's definitely a part of me. It's hard to say how much. I read somewhere—I think it was in that John Barth novel *Lost in the Funhouse*—that you should use the first person only if it's a character not at all resembling you. And I was like, Wow, I definitely broke that rule. Because Frank *is* like me. I mean, the sort of disaffected attitude. And his reactions to things. I'd say he's a version of me. Though I never did any of the things Frank did in the book, I'd say I definitely have felt like Frank did. I probably wouldn't have written the book if I hadn't. But what do you think? You're in as good a position as anyone to make a judgment on that.

DM: Well, I see characteristics that are similar. I mean, particularly that Frank is not someone that's really big on explanation. If asked, he'll answer honestly, but he's not elaborating on his feelings. And that resembles you. But he resembles other people, too. I mean, a lot of people we knew at the station were like Frank. You even stole one of my stories and gave it to him.

SB: Which one?

DM: The one where the dog eats the guy's head.

SB: Oh, yeah, that is in there. But in the final version I ended up taking out the money shot. I just have the elements. I mean, the dog, the legs of the dead person, and Frank coming in. But we don't see what he sees. I thought it was gratuitous. So I took it out. I just have him taking the picture.

DM: Did you ever take pictures yourself? I mean, on the job?

SB: No. But I know you did. I remember that you did.

DM: Well, that's true. I did take pictures for a while. I never got totally into it, though. At first I thought, Well, I'm here, I'm witnessing it, why not take a picture? Then after a while, it just becomes . . . common. I mean, how many decomposed bodies do you need to see? Blown-up cow heads and engorged tongues and the flies. After a while you're like, Yeah, all right, that's what it looks like. . . . But you never did it?

SB: No.

DM: But you chose that as a trait of your main character. Did you do that because you knew that taking pictures would be a window into Frank, who wasn't exactly tipping his hand emotionally?

SB: Definitely. It was for that specific reason. And I don't want to say it's contrived, because I like the way it turned out. But I knew exactly why I was putting that in when I did it. The book is very unusual for a first-person narrative in that there is almost no interior monologue, and the pictures sort of took the place of that. I knew they were going to serve as a window, as you say, into Frank's emotional life. And if you look at Frank's pictures of Emily, they present a very distinct progression, from him saying he won't take a picture of her, to taking a shot of her when she's fencing and she has her mask on, to taking a picture of her from far away out near the abandoned warehouse, and then, near the end, with Hock cajoling him to do it, he finally takes the portrait. And you remember there's one more photograph at the very end. He just takes a picture of her eyes. And so the whole thing is a really careful, step-by-step progression, Frank getting closer and closer to her. And I think the reader feels that progression, whether or not he's aware of it consciously.

DM: Did anyone in your family make it into the book? Like, does your relationship with your wife have anything to do with Emily?

SB: Well, not really. I mean, Amy doesn't have HIV, and she's not dying or anything. And remember, I'd started writing the book before I met Amy, and by the time I really knew Amy, the character of Emily was pretty solidified. I remember the first time Amy came over to my apartment, there was a draft of the book on the windowsill. She's really critical about literature, and apparently she peeked at the first page when I wasn't in the room. Later on she said she was relieved because she'd decided I was a good writer, and if I wasn't, she knew it wouldn't work out between us.

DM: Nice.

SB: Yeah, romance.

DM: So. One last question. Though maybe this should have been the first question. *Safelight.* The title. What were you thinking?

SB: It's the light that doesn't expose the film in the darkroom. It's the place where Frank can look at this gruesome stuff without it having any effect. You know, he has this memory of his father, he doesn't want to think about it or talk about it, but he goes into this darkroom, turns on the red light, and he can sort of experience it without having it totally overwhelm him. It's the safe representation, the echo, of what he felt. It's the first step toward him dealing with it. I think that was my idea. But remember, the original title was *The Darkroom*. It was that for a long time. And it was a long time before I decided that *Safelight* was the right title.

DM: *Safelight*'s infinitely better. To me it makes ten times more sense on every level. *The Darkroom* is a bit bleak, which is exactly what you don't want. That's where you start, but that's not where you finish, and that's not what the book is about.

SB: Well, I hope that's true.

DM: Looking back, and now that it's done, out of your hands, the errors are there, you can't fix it, can't change it, it's out there for all of mankind to peruse for eternity, are there things about it you'd change or that you're not satisfied with?

SB: There are definitely lines that I think could have been better written. There are places where I used the same word twice on the same page. There are one or two scenes that I might have taken out. But in general I'm happy with the book, though I do wish I was a better writer when I wrote it.

DM: Oh, come on, man.

SB: But I'm not saying I'm displeased. I feel good about the book. I think it says what I wanted it to say. I'm proud of it.

DM: Well, you should be. You captured the emotional nature of the job better than anything else I've ever seen written. I mean, what people like us went through, and how people really reacted.

SB: Rather than perpetuating the myth?

DM: Yeah, exactly. Catch the baby from the burning window—that sort of bullshit. For me, the book captures exactly what it's like to work as an EMT in a place like New York. It's not something I've seen anywhere else.

1. The name Frank draws attention to the narrator's dogged insistence on telling the truth. It also relates to his photographic subject matter and the world in which he lives. Reflect further upon the name Frank as it illuminates his character and response to life. In addition, discuss possible meanings of other characters' names. For example, how might Emily's last name, Pascal, add richness to your understanding of her circumstances and choices? Discuss the names of other central characters, such as Norman, Hock, and Burnett, and how the names might shed light on what these people mean to Frank and on the larger issues raised by the novel.

2. Frank's troubled relationship with his brother, Norman, is a thread running through the novel. Develop a portrait of Norman's childhood, his relationship with Frank and his father, his decision to become a surgeon, and the quality of his present life. How does Norman feel about Frank? What does Frank want from Norman? Discuss how their relationship evolves in the novel. Near the end of the novel, Frank decides not to tell Norman that his father would have wanted to see him. Does this deliberate omission suggest that Frank continues to resent his brother or that he has hope for their relationship?

3. Frank seeks acceptance and approval from Norman, but also from other men in his life. Compare Burnett to Norman. Compare Hock to Norman.

4. Certain characters function as wisdom figures for Frank. What life lessons does Frank learn from the Tylenol patient, the blind man, the burned man, Bontecou, and other characters?

5. Gil Hock is a paradoxical character. On the one hand, he is a corrupting influence on Frank, and on the other hand, he is a benevolent advisor and friend. To what extent do Hock's contradictions mirror untenable contradictions in Frank's own moral perspective?

6. The descriptive passages chronicling industrial waste and urban decay create an apocalyptic landscape of despair. Against this backdrop, the reader expects to read about illness, death, corruption, and brutality. It is surprising that the narrator discovers and preserves beauty within this world. Cite particular vignettes in which beauty arises from the grotesque, and compare those instances in order to identify common origins and expressions of beauty in the novel.

7. In the novel, urban industrial settings are contrasted with natural settings. Emily describes natural beauty as "hollow" (p. 184). Does Frank respond to natural beauty in the same way Emily does? What seems to be missing from natural beauty for both Emily and Frank? Where does beauty lie for each of them?

8. Repeatedly, Frank describes himself as being ashamed. What is Frank ashamed of, and how does he respond to his shame?

9. What role does the subject of suicide play in the novel? How do the suicides that Frank witnesses as a paramedic relate to his own experience of having witnessed the aftermath of his father's suicide? Is Frank suicidal? By the end of the novel, has Frank embraced life or is he still "on the edge"?

10. How do you respond to the portraits of paramedics, policemen, and doctors in this novel? Does viewing the protectors and healers of society as corrupt and flawed cause you to feel anxiety, revulsion, or hostility toward society, or toward the novel itself?

11. Explain why Frank becomes involved in the first and subsequent drug deals. How does his decision to become involved in crimes make you feel about him? Do you hold him responsible or view him as a victim?

12. Hock wants Frank's photographs for his own gain, but he also seems to understand and appreciate Frank's obsession. What does Hock seek in the photographs?

13. Analyze Frank's motives in creating the pictures. How do the photographs provide Frank with a medium for processing his experience? Is Frank an artist or a journalist? How do the descriptions of Frank's photographs function in the novel? Are they gratuitous? How do the photographs change as the novel goes on?

14. Trace the evolution of Frank's approach to his photographs. Does he develop as an artist or does he sacrifice his artistic integrity in order to survive in the world?

15. When Frank finally photographs Emily, near the end of her life, he knows that he has taken a portrait of "something beautiful" (p. 192). What beautiful thing has Frank seen and recorded for others to see?

16. By the end of the novel, to what extent has Frank found safety and light? Connect the term "safelight" from photography with Frank's search for meaning.

17. In a novel in which the narrator is chronically inarticulate, the wisdom figures are corrupt and coercive, and the images are horrifying and tragic, is it appropriate to reach for a higher meaning or theme? If you could speak for (or to) Frank, how would you phrase a central theme for this novel?

18. Ultimately, what is the tone of the novel—that is, does the author speak in a voice of hope or a voice of despair? Does Frank grow as a human being or deteriorate? Does Emily's spirit live on (as she wants to believe) or is her death (and her separation from Frank) final? Is Frank and Emily's doomed love affair evidence of the tenacity of the human condition or of its fragility? Are Frank's photographs an act of creative renewal or expressions of life's futility?

SHANNON BURKE is a novelist and screenwriter. Before moving to his current home in Knoxville, he worked as a paramedic in Harlem and lived in Chicago, Chapel Hill, New Orleans, Los Angeles, and Mexico. *Safelight* is his first novel.

About the Type

This book was set in Fairfield, the first typeface from the hand of the distinguished American artist and engraver Rudolph Ruzicka (1883–1978). In its structure Fairfield displays the sober and sane qualities of the master craftsman whose talent has long been dedicated to clarity. It is this trait that accounts for the trim grace and vigor, the spirited design and sensitive balance, of this original typeface.

Rudolph Ruzicka was born in Bohemia and came to America in 1894. He set up his own shop, devoted to wood engraving and printing, in New York in 1913 after a varied career working as a wood engraver, in photoengraving and banknote printing plants, and as an art director and freelance artist. He designed and illustrated many books, and was the creator of a considerable list of individual prints—wood engravings, line engravings on copper, and aquatints.